THE PONDERS

THE PONDERS

Norah M. Field

The Book Guild Ltd
Sussex, England

This book is a work of fiction. The characters and situations in this story are imaginary. No resemblance is intended between these characters and any real persons, either living or dead.

The Book Guild Limited
Temple House
25 High Street
Lewes, Sussex

First published 1990

Set in Baskerville

Typesetting by Book Economy Services
Burgess Hill

Printed in Great Britain by
Antony Rowe Ltd
Chippenham

British Library Cataloguing in Publication Data
Field, Norah
The Ponders
I. Title
823'.914 [F]

ISBN 0 86332 482 7

To my husband, Reg,
with very many thanks
for all his help and encouragement

Contents

Glossary

APOTHECARY – a chemist or doctor.
BURIAT – rough woollen cloth.
BUSKINS – boots worn by countrymen.
CAMLET – material of wool or goat's hair.
CAPA – a hooded cloak.
CHAPERON – a hood.
CHIN CLOUT – a kerchief to wrap round the mouth in cold weather.
CLOUT – a kerchief or napkin.
COIF – a bonnet worn by country women.
CORDWAINER – a shoemaker.
DOWLAS – linen for shirts and aprons.
DUFFEL – coarse woollen cloth, often blue or scarlet.
DURANCE – material for petticoats for women.
ELL – an old measure of 45 inches.
FRIEZE – coarse woollen cloth for jerkins, doublets and gowns.
FRUMENTY – porridge made from wheat.
GALLIARD – a quick, lively dance.
GALLIMAUFRY – a hash made of odds and ends of food.
HOSE – breeches.
HOSEN – stockings.
INKLE – a narrow tape for trimming hats or dresses-often yellow.
KERSEY – coarse woollen cloth.
KIRTLE – a skirt or loose gown.

PATTENS	–	wooden shoes or clogs.
PAVAN	–	a grave, stately dance.
PINNER	–	an apron with a bib.
PIPKIN	–	a cup.
PLATTER	–	a plate.
PURITANS	–	English Protestants in the 16th and 17th centuries who wanted simpler forms of worship, and strictness and gravity in behaviour.
SKILLET	–	a long handled pan.
SLOUGH	–	a swampy place.
STAMMEL	–	a red cloth.
STICKEN PINS	–	knitting needles.
STICKLE	–	a stick.
SUGAR-LOAF	–	a solid cone-shaped mass of sugar sold in former times which also gave its name to hats of the same shape.
SWAILE	–	an old name for the 'shade'.
VOLTA or LAVOLTA	–	a lively dance.

CHAPTER

1

Northampton Gaol,1649.

Beth *John* *Charley*

The wicket gate of the prison slammed shut and three frightened children stood close together on the inside of Northampton's grim gaol, in a courtyard surrounded by dark, formidable walls. A fierce gaoler scowled down at them.

'So you want to see your father?' His thick brows came together.

'If it please you sir.'

He was the oldest of the three who spoke a coppery-headed, freckled boy of fourteen or so in the knee breeches, the Cossack-style coat with its bib collar and the 'sugar loaf' hat of a Puritan.

'Name?'

'John.'

'Not yours - Your father's.'

'Ponder - Nathaniel Ponder.'

'Ponder - Ponder - I know him. What's he in for?' he growled.

'Holding prayer meetings sir.'

'Prayer meetings,' there was a sneer in his voice. 'One'o them Puritans eh? - or whatever they calls themselves, who won't conform to what every other good Christian does. Well, they knows the law - no religious meetings outside the church, if they breaks it, so much the worse for them. He could be out tomorrow if he'd promise to stop his preaching. I dunno about you visiting him. Where's your mother?'

'We haven't got one - she's dead.'

'Who looks arter yer?'

'We look after each other.'

The hard face relaxed a little. He had children of his own.

'Who are these?'

'My younger sister Beth and my little brother Charley.

He scowled, looking from one to the other. That girl, Beth, would be about the same age as his own daughter.

'Follow me.' he grunted. He was powerfully built and his gruff voice, black beard and long black hair frightened Beth.

'You'll probably find him on his knees a-praying. He ought ter be praying for forgiveness, leaving young 'uns like you ter fend for yerselves.' He turned and strode ahead, his great keys clanking – the keys that opened the massive oak doors studded with iron, creaking as they swung back and groaning rustily as they crashed behind them.

They followed him along endless passages, dark, damp loathsome places that seemed to twist and turn in all directions. They looked around fearfully and kept close to each other. 'Are there hobgoblins in here?' Charley whispered.

'No,' Beth whispered back, 'they're in the woods.'

At last they stopped before another door, the same as all the rest except it had a small grating near the top. They could hear an uproar within.

The gaoler peered through then opened the door slightly. 'He's in there,' he said giving them a push. 'I'll give you ten minutes.'

There was a sudden hush as the door banged shut and the great key turned. They were locked in.

At first it was difficult to discern anything in the half light. There was a stench of dampness, dirt and the sour smell of rotting rushes on the floor. The din had started again and they could dimly see bodies – some fighting, some lying on the floor groaning, some rocking endlessly to and fro, some frighteningly close, whose faces leered into theirs. Some thrust out their hands shouting for food. Most were in rags and tatters.

Then they saw their father on his knees praying, just as the gaoler had said. He looked unwashed and unkempt, quite oblivious of the uproar all around him. Falling, stepping over, dodging the noisy ragamuffins, they reached him.

'Father! Father!' they cried.

'My children!' He rose, tall, strong-boned, and turned toward them, his face shining as one who had suddenly awakened from a wonderful dream. Beth buried her head in his shoulder and he stroked the red-gold hair that fell from under her white coif.

'My little Marybud,' that was his pet name for her, and she loved it. John stood silent, while young Charley pushed in to say they had some baby rabbits.

'Oh, father,' Beth looked around fearfully, 'leave this dreadful place – the gaoler said you could come home tomorrow if you would promise to stop the prayer meetings. Thou art a good man father but you can be just as good if you go to church like everybody else.'

'I may be only a poor village shoemaker, but no priest shall come between me and my God – nor will I bow the knee in church. I have an inner light. I can speak to Him and He to me. I am nearer to Him in this 'dreadful place' as you call it, than in all the great churches of the land. Besides, I can help these poor souls by giving them courage and hope.'

'But what of us father? What shall we do? How are we to live?'

'Live? Live?'. He sounded surprised. 'Thou must have faith.' There was a brightness in his voice. 'There is a little money in my special wooden box that ye know of, I am making shoe laces for you to sell, you have the garden to grow vegetables, and the rabbits will multiply. There are the woods close by with their wild fruits and nuts and plenty of kindling for the fire. There is nothing for thee to fear or worry about. Talk to God as a friend – He will supply all your needs – ask and ye will receive.'

The gaoler was at the door again. They had only time for a quick farewell. 'God bless you my children. Here are the laces, take them as you go. My prayers and thoughts are with you often. I hope yours are with me.'

They fought their way through clamorous bodies and were pulled out again.

'Well, did yer manage to persuade him to do no more preaching.'

Beth shook her head sadly. 'Then he'll surely be in for a twelvemonth.'

Before long the wicket gate of the prison slammed shut again. This time they were on the outside, on their own, alone. The gaoler had said, 'for a twelvemonth'. He might just as well have said ten or twenty twelve-months, so far away did the end of that year seem.

It was a bitter February day and they were cold and dispirited as they set off back. It was fourteen miles along the lanes and by-ways to Rowell, the small village where they lived in a thatched ironstone cottage in Meadow Lane, a cottage owned by Sir Aldwig Du Vayne, the Lord of the Manor, who in fact owned all the village and the farm lands round about. The low sun sent dazzling shafts of light on to a frozen waste of white but there was no warmth in it, it could not fight the bitter

NORTH·AMPTON
GAOL

cold. The recent snow had been whipped into deep ridges and drifts and the biting wind said there was more to come. They walked sharply, ran sometimes, to get warm and presently their fingers and toes glowed and their cheeks tingled. It felt good to be away from that dreadful prison – perhaps life would not be so bad after all.

Charley had been unusually subdued but now he began to run, to crunch the icy grasses under his feet and try to splinter the frozen sloughs with his heels or slide on them. A tall blackthorn, gorse or bramble copse gave them welcome shelter now and again from the cutting wind. From time to time they spotted an owl as it found its hole in a willow; long-tailed tits searching for lost berries; a cock pheasant strutting, but always just out of reach, or a covey of partridges whirring past. Here and there a cow or heavily fleeced sheep turned and peered curiously at them.

If they left the road and took a short cut from one village to the next, the only signs to guide them were the spires of the churches or in some places the canvas sails of a post-mill. As long as they kept these in sight they knew they were heading in the right direction. If they slackened pace the cold took grip once more. Beth pulled her russet capa more tightly about her kirtle, John tightened the belt of his coat while Charley pulled up his worsted hose to meet his knee breeches and pulled down his round cap to stop the frost from biting his ears. They sang all the tunes they knew to keep their feet marching and Charley whistled to them with no tune at all.

'God bless thee Charley, if thee must whistle, then whistle in tune,' Beth grumbled; ''tis like the shriek of the wind in the chimney.'

'Tell us a story then,' said Charley and Beth told some of her favourites that he had often heard before. They were about hobgoblins and the foul fiends who lived in the woods, whom she had *almost* seen many times when she was nutting or sticking; and about the fairies who came out when the pale silver moon shone and danced in the green fairy rings. But the ones Charley liked best were tales of Troy or of King Arthur and his Knights, that were in some of their father's chap-books – for Nathaniel had taught both Beth and John to read.

'I'll tell you one,' said John, 'it's about a man who went to the stables to hire a horse.

'This is a religious one,' said the ostler.

'A religious one?' the man questioned.

'Yes,' replied the ostler, 'when you want him to go, shout "GOD BE PRAISED! GOD BE PRAISED!" and when you want him to stop shout "ALLELUIA".'

So the man mounted and cried loudly, 'GOD BE PRAISED! GOD BE PRAISED!'

Sure enough the horse went trotting off at a good pace. After a time, however, he noticed he was coming to a deep ravine. Very alarmed he cried out loudly, 'ALLELUIA! ALLELUIA!' Just as the ostler had said, the horse stopped – right on the very edge. The man wiped his brow and breathing a great sigh of relief, he put his hands together and looking up

After a time, however, he noticed he was coming to a deep ravine. Very alarmed he cried out loudly, 'Alleluia! Alleluia! Alleluia!'

to Heaven muttered fervently, 'GOD BE PRAISED! GOD BE PRAISED!'

'And what happened?' said Charley.

'What do you think?' John chuckled.

They all laughed as Charley saw the jest and then with mock severity Beth chided, ' 'Tis sinful of you John to use holy words thus. Our father would not approve.'

'Our father uses the very same words every day,' John smiled, and they all laughed again while Charley went bounding ahead pretending to be the man on the horse, falling down when he came to the 'ravine'.

'Thou are a pest,' scolded Beth, 'all thy clothes will be wet and dirty.'

Brixworth, Broughton Green, Cransley, Loddington, then the farm called Three Chimneys and they knew they were getting towards Rowell and home – only a mile or so to go. A long tree lay across their path half covered with snow.

'Let's take it home and I'll cut it up for firewood,' said John. So they each took a hold and dragged it along and over the snow, leaving a trail behind them.

The short February day was darkening and as they trudged down the steep hill from Three Chimneys and came towards Rowell, they could see the lights in the cottages twinkling like sequins on a black dress.

Where Loddington Road joined Kettering Road, they could hear a rowdy crowd yelling and shouting. The ugly voice of a mob always frightened Beth so they dropped the branch by the roadside and hid under Pack-horse Bridge over Slade Brook.

'Don't worry,' John whispered, ' 'tis only a market crowd coming from Kettering with too much ale in their bellies,' and before long they had passed still fighting as they went up into Rowell. The children followed at a safe distance and before long reached Meadow Lane and their own little cottage.

'Home at last!' said Beth thankfully as they dropped the heavy branch down by the door. There was something comforting about that word 'Home.'

John struggled with the tinder box for a while and presently a rush dip glimmered in the darkness and then another and before long a fire of small sticks was crackling merrily on the

'Home at last!' said Beth thankfully as they dropped the heavy branch down by the door.

stone hearth as Charley worked energetically with the bellows.

'Gently Charley, not too hard,' Beth called laying out platters and spoons on the wooden table. As two or three bigger logs were thrown on, they spluttered and sparked and the smooth flames leaped up and threw their light and warmth into the room and onto the leaded windows, white with frost.

They were warm now and soon hungrily eating the gallimaufry, a hash of odds and ends of food heated over the fire in a skillet. The dips sent up little spirals of smoke and threw grotesque shadows through the haze onto the walls hung with dried herbs and onions.

When they had eaten John and Beth sat on the rough wooden stools and Charley on the floor rushes holding out their hands to the warm glow, gazing with wind-beaten and fire-burnt faces into the flames and rubbing their itching chilblains. Beside the fire was a wooden settle. It stood empty now for none of them would have thought of sitting on it. It was their father's and its emptiness reminded them of him. It was one of their favourite pastimes on winter evenings when the work was done, to sit round the hearth and look for 'fire – pictures'.

'What can you see John?'

'King Arthur and his knights all dressed in red and fighting, and a goblin jumping up and down and yelling.'

'And see, right in there,' said Beth pointing, 'there's a beautiful maiden in the middle of the flames being burned to death. Look – you can see her – oh, she's gone to ashes!'

'Your turn Charley,' said John. But Charley was curled up on the rushes almost asleep.

'It's good to be home,' sighed Beth, 'but I wish father was here. I wonder what he's doing now and if he's thinking of us.'

'Probably on his knees a-praying as the gaoler said.'

Beth nodded.

'Time for bed Charley!'

She pushed him halfway up the wooden stairs that led from their one living room. The rest he crawled on his hands and knees still half asleep.

A cold, frozen moon looked down on the little cottage in

Meadow Lane as John fetched in another couple of logs and threw them, crackling sparks, onto the fire. Beth cleared away the wooden platters and washed them and the skillet.

'Frumenty will be good for breakfast,' she thought as she put a handful of wheat into a dish of water and placed it in the warm bread oven by the side of the fire. By morning it would have swelled into a thick porridge.

Meanwhile John had fetched his father's wooden box. It was indeed a very special box. It had been Nathaniel's father's and his father's before that, so nobody knew where it came from in the first place. Underneath was carved 'N. PONDER' for there had been a Nathaniel in the family for generations. It was quite small but the strange thing about it was that it had a secret lock and a tiny key and nobody was able to open it until they had been carefully shown, for the key had to be turned three times forward and twice backwards before it would open. Nathaniel had told its secret to John and now *he* told it to Beth. She tried several times before she got the knack of it. There was not very much inside but as the lid sprang back it revealed a piece of white linen and wrapped in it was their mother's wedding ring and a small cross she had in her hand when she died. As their father had said, there was also some money, enough to pay next half year's rent when it fell due in June and a small amount besides for food they must buy.

John looked despondent but Beth, always the optimist, reminded him that their father had said God would supply all their needs.

'We can sell the shoe laces in Kettering on market day,' she went on, 'and then there's Rowell Fair and Desborough Feast, besides all the other fairs, feasts and mops round about, which will help, and when Spring and Summer comes perhaps Farmer Thacker will give thee a job for he is sure to need extra help with haymaking and harvest.'

John nodded slowly. 'We'd better hide this box somewhere,' he said, 'somewhere that only thee and me know of.'

Beth suggested there was a loose stone up the chimney but John thought that might be dangerous if they had a blazing fire. Under the floor was no good for that was only hardened mud with rushes on top. 'Upstairs?' said Beth pondering, and

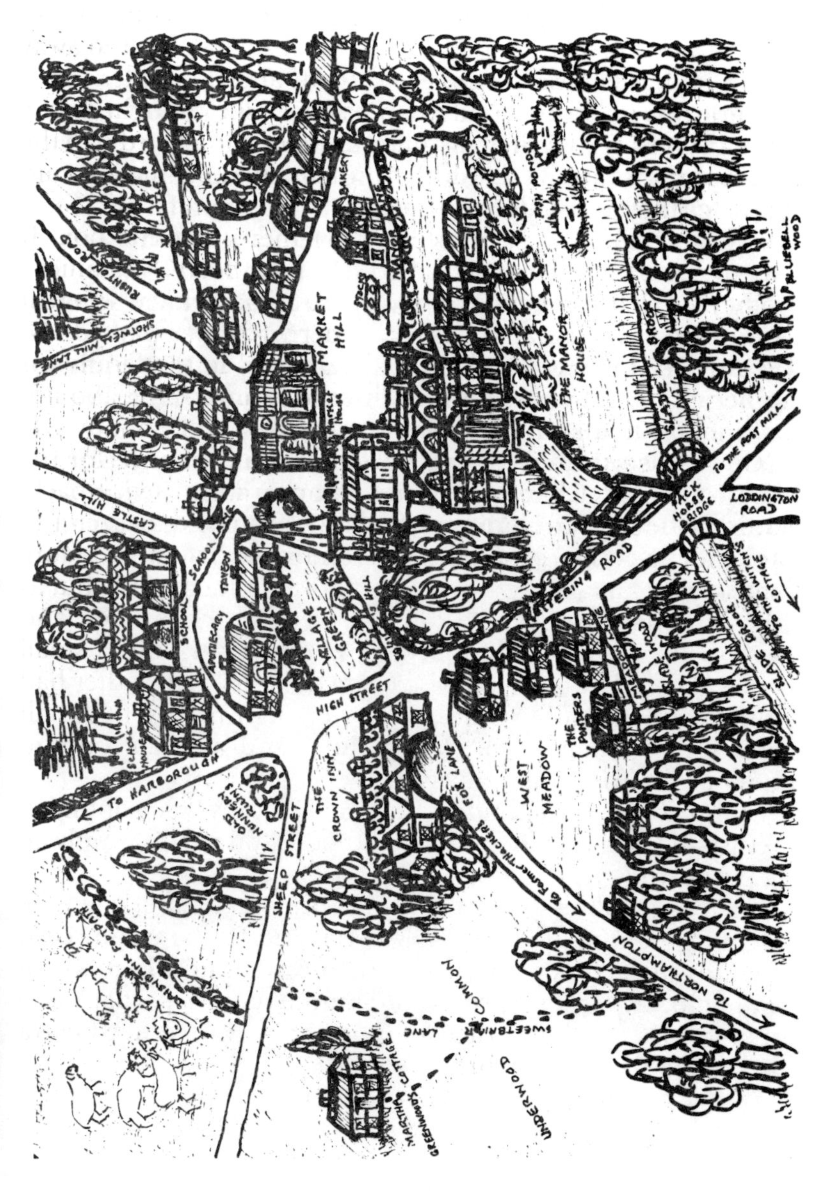
RUNTON ROAD
MARKET HILL
BAKERY
STOCKS
FISH PONDS
THE MANOR HOUSE
SLADE BROOK
BLUEBELL WOOD
TO THE POST MILL
LODDINGTON ROAD
PACK HORSE BRIDGE
MARKET HOUSE
CASTLE HILL
SCHOOL LANE
SCHOOL
TAVERN
APOTHECARY
VILLAGE GREEN
HIGH STREET
SCHOOL HOUSE
TO HARBOROUGH
OLD NUNNERY RUINS
SHEEP STREET
THE CROWN INN
FOX LANE
WEST MEADOW
THE PINDERS
MEADOW LANE
TO NORTHAMPTON
COMMON
SWEETBRIAR LANE
UNDERWOOD
MARTHA'S COTTAGE

Rowell

then strangely enough they both thought of the same place together.

'On top of the wall!'

There was really only one room upstairs but a wooden partition divided it in half. This partition went nearly up to the sloping rafters but not quite, leaving a little ledge. So it was on this ledge they decided to put the box. They thought it wiser to say nothing about it to Charley, scatter-brain that he was.

Between themselves they called it the 'Hidey Box'.

They had had a long day and were tired for they had set out to Northampton at day-break that morning, so they fastened the door (but not before Beth had put out a last bit of their supper – a 'Good piece' for the fairies) raked out the ashes of the fire and thankfully tumbled into bed.

'God bless father tonight in Northampton Gaol and please bless John and Charley and me, Amen,' were Beth's last words as she pushed from her mind the grim memories of the day and left the problems of tomorrow to look after themselves.

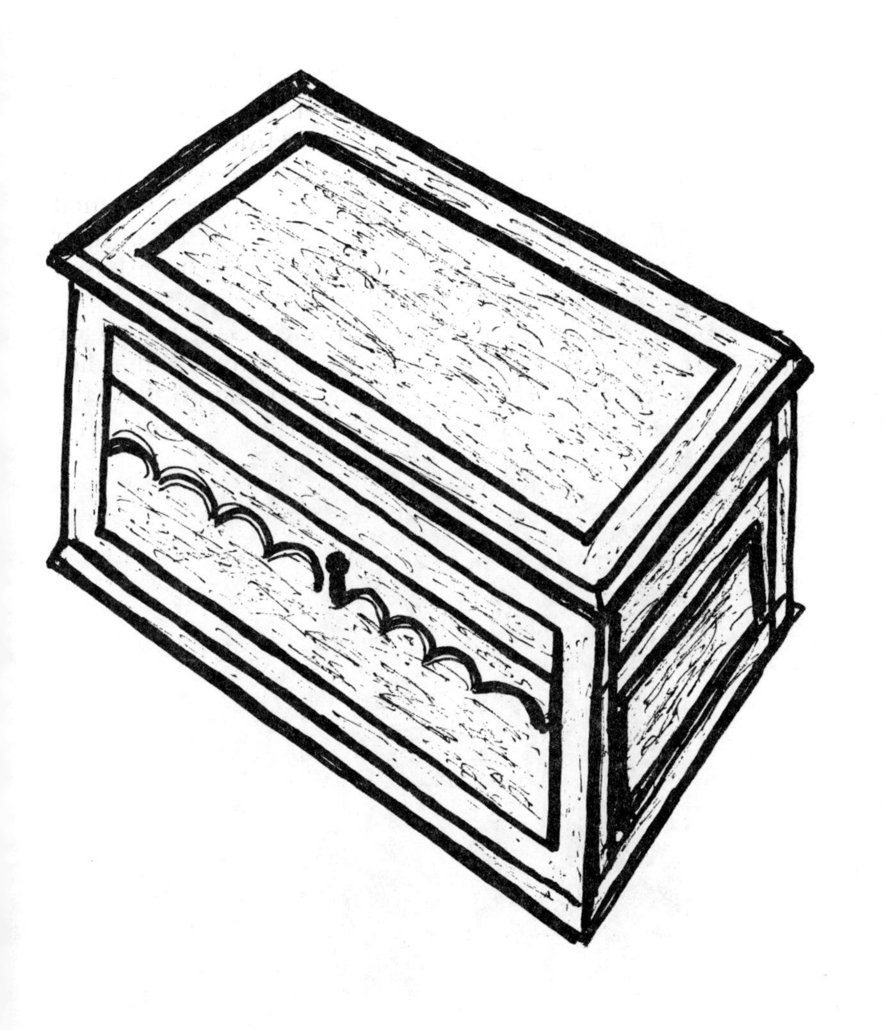

The 'Hidey Box'

CHAPTER

2

Bailiff Foggarty comes for the rent.
Kettering Market.
Sammy and his mother, Martha Greenwood.

It was the drumming of wooden pattens on the roadway and the rumbling of cart wheels over the cobbles that woke them next morning.

Beth breathed on the diamond-shaped panes and rubbed. There was still a big white world outside. She put on her grey working kirtle and canvas pinner and ladled out the frumenty onto the wooden platters. It had soaked up the water during the night and now Beth added a little milk to the thick pudding. That and some coarse brown bread made their meal.

Firewood was always a problem so John decided his first job was to saw up the branch they had dragged home last night and Charley was put to stack the logs and collect the small bits in the old rush basket for kindling. Their breath rose like smoke on the frosty air as they puffed at their labours by the back of the house.

Beth had some washing and mending to do and wondered what they could have for their next meal. John settled it.

'I have killed one of the rabbits,' he said as he hung it just inside the back door.

All at once there was a commotion outside and a booming voice shouting. The front latch was jerked up and the door banged open. 'Ten thousand hells confound you! Why the devil can't yer knock them icicles down off yer roof – they're as long as me arm and as deadly as a sword – they might'a blinded me!'

In marched the burly figure of Master Foggarty, Sir Aldwig Du Vayne's bailiff, his cocked hat knocked off by the icicle, exposing his egg-bald head to the winter wind.

Without as much as 'By your leave', he came in, his short-sighted eyes peering about him as he strutted round the room, hat in one hand and a thick oak stick in the other.

The bulbous nose sniffed at the iron pot hanging over the fire but there was nothing in it except water and some herbs. His heavy, protruding lower lip watered however as he smelled the onion. He had pried like this before and always said something about 'It's amazing how much food the poor manage to get.' This time he could see nothing and having peered around he seated himself on their father's settle and replaced his cocked hat. Working for Sir Aldwig as he did, he half fancied he *was* Sir Aldwig, for he emulated his dress almost to the last button in a cheaper sort of way. The one

In marched the burly figure of Bailiff Foggarty.
'Ten thousand hells confound you! Why the devil can't yer knock them icicles down off yer roof – they're as deadly as a sword – they might'a blinded me!'

thing he could not emulate was the Squire's long curled hair, for *he* was as bald as a coot. Sitting there in his calf-length top coat with its wide cuffs, he stuck out his legs showing his rolled-up stockings and buckled shoes, and his ample stomach displayed his long waistcoat buttoned from top to bottom almost covering his full breeches. Having adjusted the hat to his satisfaction, he banged his stick on the ground.

'Where's that no-good brother of yours?' he demanded.

'Out at the back sir, chopping wood.'

He got up and strutted towards the door. With his nose in the air as usual, again trying to imitate the Lord of the Manor, he did not see one of the heavy stools in his path and walked right into it.

'The devil confound you!' he exploded; 'A plague on me gouty leg.' He rubbed his shins. 'Ah, a pretty sight indeed,' he added as he spotted the dead rabbit. 'So, this is how the poor live! It 'ud be water gruel if I had my way. Where'd yer say yer brother was?'

'Outside sir, if it please you sir.'

He flung open the door with a bang. 'Confound you, where the devil are you? – Oblige me by stepping inside will you?'

'That I will sir, I did not know you were here.' John's voice was quietly calm. Bailiff Foggarty eyed him up and down.

'What I want to know young fellow is, now that your father's in prison, how do you Puritan Ponders intend to pay your rent?'

'Oh,' said John quietly, 'is that all – I thought something was amiss.'

'Amiss! Amiss!' The bailiff detected a note of defiance in John's voice. 'Something soon will be my spirited young game cock if your rent's not paid on time.'

'Never fear thee, Sir Aldwig's rent *will* be paid on time – the next half-year's is not due until June so in the meanwhile, by your leave sir, perhaps we may be left in peace.' So saying he moved to the front door and opened it. 'Give you good-day sir,' he said looking straight ahead of him.

Bailiff Fogarty was somewhat abashed by John's coolness and stood for a minute looking from him to Beth and back again before he exploded, 'Bah! The devil take you,' and catching sight of the dead rabbit, 'a pretty sight indeed!'

He was barely through the door however, when Wham! a snowball hit him squarely on the head and again the cocked hat lay in the slush.

It was Charley, who, having finished his labours with the wood was testing his aim with a pile of snowballs.

'Confound you, you young devil – you did that on purpose!'

Charley was genuinely amazed. 'No sir, if you please sir, I didn't know you were coming out of the door just then sir.'

In that split second of surprise Bailiff Foggarty saw his chance and lifting his stick, brought it down sharply on Charley's back and shoulders. 'That'll teach yer, yer scurvy rascal!'

The stick came down again but Charley had dodged through the open door and it swiped fruitlessly at the empty air.

'Yer no-good son of a felon,' he muttered. His scowling brows came down over his eyes. 'And you'll feel my stickle again if yer come within an ell of me never fear!' Was his parting shot as he polished his bare head with a kerchief and replaced the hat once more. John and Beth were standing outside and the last they heard of him as he strode off was, 'A plague on me gouty leg!'

John made sure he was gone then stepped inside and shut the door. He looked serious but Beth collapsed with mirth onto one of the stools.

'He looked so funny with his bald head like a big shiny egg,' she spluttered, and Charley crawled out from under the table where he had been hiding and hobbled about imitating the Bailiff's voice,

'A plague on me gouty leg! A plague on me gouty leg! But really Beth, my back does hurt where his stickle hit me.'

'Never mind, chuck,' said Beth giving it a rub, 'I'll put some comfrey ointment on it.'

Then Beth too looked serious. 'He would love to be able to turn us out John on some excuse or other.'

'Maybe,' her brother replied quietly, 'but he can't, so long as we pay the rent at the proper time. We must always keep enough money for that. I think we should go to Kettering next market day and see if we can sell some of the laces.'

Accordingly one morning about a week later, John and Beth set off the four miles to the town leaving some small tasks for Charley to do while they were away. The snow was disappearing but it was a cold, raw day and the market traders under the arches of the Town Hall were having a poor time of it, stamping their feet and banging their arms to keep warm.

The shops too with their creaking signs and open fronts – the confectioner's, the tailor's, the saddler's, the candlemaker's, the soap-boiler's, the glover's, the meal man, the chicken man, the barber – were not very busy for nobody had travelled there if they could avoid it and it was all John and Beth could do to sell half a dozen pairs of laces at two farthings a pair.

A baker was shivering in the stocks with some stale and mouldy loaves around him. 'Must have been giving short weight,' John observed.

Dogs scavenged the street for food and beggars hung around the ale houses where men were drinking and gambling, singing and shouting. Women out shopping clattered by in their pattens, picking their way through the slush and taking no notice of two children selling laces.

Beth shivered and pulled her capa round her and John tied his muffler tighter round his mouth. 'We'll sell no more laces today,' he said.

They passed a butcher's stall. Stewing mutton was four pence the pound. We could afford a half,' said Beth looking at their twelve farthings.

'Hey you, you, get yer thieving eyes and hands off me stall, d'ye hear?' the butcher bawled seeing them, heads together, deciding what to buy.

'We don't steal.' There was always a quiet dignity about John when he was angry.

'If you please sir, half a pound of your stewing mutton,' said Beth.

'Ugh!' He looked them up and down. 'Show us yer money then.' Beth held out eight farthings.

He peered at them again. They did not seem like the usual run of thieves. Perhaps he had been a bit hasty – they looked cold and hungry. 'I ain't in business to feed beggars yer know, but there's a bit extra for yer,' and he dobbed another small piece on top. Beth thanked him and they walked on.

'The chicken man's eggs are three a penny,' said John, 'one each.' They placed them carefully in the basket and set off back.

Walking was difficult on the slushy road and Beth was glad it was only four miles and not the fourteen they had had to treck from Northampton.

As they neared Rowell and were going down Windmill Hill towards the pack-horse bridge over Slade Brook, they began to hear unusual sounds which made them stop, look at each other, and listen. Somewhere ahead of them there was a confused noise of loud shouts and raucous laughter, and above all the din came the sound of yells and screams. Beth was frightened, mobs, drunkards and apprentices fighting always scared her but John pushed on and she followed slowly at a distance.

To their left as they came down the hill was a very high bank with trees behind it. On top of this bank was an ungainly lad, thin as a sapling but tall as a grown man, in a peasant smock with cock feathers stuck in his old cap. He was apparently in a violent rage, for he jumped about like a wild ape, yelling and pulling grotesque faces. Beth wondered if he really was a human being. He grabbed at stones and clods of earth and threw them at a crowd of boys who were on the road below him. They in their turn were pelting and jeering at him.

'Sammy, Sammy, where's yer mammy!' they roared out together.

'Old Sammy Greenwood is no good, chop him up for firewood,' they sang in chorus. A large stone hit Sammy full on the forehead and blood began to pour down his face and onto his smock.

'It's Silly Sammy,' said John, 'and the village boys are tormenting him – they love to do that – and what's more, there's our Charley among them!'

At that moment Charley caught sight of them and let fall the stone he was just about to fling.

'Charley!' He knew that tone of Beth's voice. She was angry with him.

'Get off you cowardly lot,' shouted John, 'you ought to be ashamed of yourselves tormenting a poor half-witted lad who's done you no harm!' Hearing John's voice and seeing the blood, they dropped the stones and turves and began to run off.

Sammy was sitting on the bank whimpering. Blood was trickling down from under his hands as he clutched his head. John climbed up to him.

'Who is he?' asked Beth.

'It's Sammy Greenwood. He lives with his widowed mother up on Underwood Common. They have only come here recently.'

'Bring him down,' she said.

'I can't make him get up.' John was struggling to help the lumbering figure to his feet.

Anyone in trouble and Beth was always ready. The rowdy crowd had vanished so she was no longer afraid. Charley had gone too, fleeing no doubt from the wrath to come.

'I'll climb up,' she said, setting down the rush basket and scrambling, with John's help, up the steep bank. Somehow, between them, they got him down on to the road, still whimpering and crying.

'Underwood Common's a good step away, perhaps we'd better take him to our house and bathe his head,' Beth suggested picking up her basket.

John thought this was a good idea and one on each side, they helped him along still stunned and dazed by the stone.

The wound was not too bad when they had washed off the blood. He was more frightened than hurt. Beth talked to him kindly and gave him an apple from the barrel in the corner, but when John told him, by signs mostly, that it was time to go home, he stamped from one foot to the other, shook his head vigorously and swung his arms from side to side shouting, 'Nar! Nar! Nar!' Poor Sammy. So little kindness had come his way that he was not willing to leave his new friends.

After a time they managed to persuade him that his mother would be worried and together they set out across West Meadow at the back of their house, along Fox Lane to Sweetbriar Footpath and from there to Martha Greenwood's cottage on Underwood Common. Martha was at the door as they approached looking anxious as she saw Sammy between them with his head bandaged.

They told her the whole story (leaving out Charley's part in it) and she was very grateful indeed for their kindness and help. Her late husband had been a ship's captain she said but two years ago his ship had been wrecked coming back from the Indies and he and all the crew had drowned. He had left her a little money and she had worked as a cook in some of the big London houses but she was born and bred in Northamptonshire and felt she should come back and live in the country so that her poor Sammy could wander about as he liked without being tormented by the London boys or apprentices. She was very distressed to learn about today's incident but happy indeed that John and Beth had been kind to him.

Sammy, too, was happy as he showed by clapping his hands, hopping from one leg to the other and making all sorts of facial contortions accompanied by his own weird noises.

Martha knew about the Ponder children and that their father was imprisoned in Northampton gaol. Her brother, she said, lived in Northampton and he too was of the Puritan faith though not a preacher. He had fought for Cromwell at the Battle of Naseby four years earlier.

She and Beth liked each other immediately and before they came away she insisted they took some of her home-made gingerbread with them and added that she would help them in any way she was able. Her kind face was smiling as she stood outside the cottage to see them off and as Beth turned to wave, her white coif and collar and her white pinner over her red stammel petticoat were silhouetted against a flaming sunset.

'Red at night, shepherd's delight – should be a nice day tomorrow,' said John, ' – and now for our Charley – if he's dared to come home by now.'

'Don't be too hard on him,' Beth begged, 'he's only a little boy.'

'He's old enough to know better than throw stones at poor defenceless creatures. He must be punished somehow.'

'Give him some extra tasks,' Beth suggested. 'You can't deny him too much – it's little enough any of us gets these days. We've only got each other and we must stick together.'

When they got home Charley was nowhere to be seen, not under the table (his usual hiding place) nor upstairs, where he had been known to hide under the bed.

A search out at the back however revealed him in the barn

where their father carried on his trade of cordwainer. John dragged him out and after a stern talk was still for sending him supperless to bed, but Beth's soft heart prevailed and they all sat down to some mutton stew and as Charley heard more of the story and enjoyed Martha's gingerbread, he was genuinely sorry for his part in the episode.

'I promise I won't do it again,' he said in a very contrite voice. So ended their little adventure with Sammy – or did it?

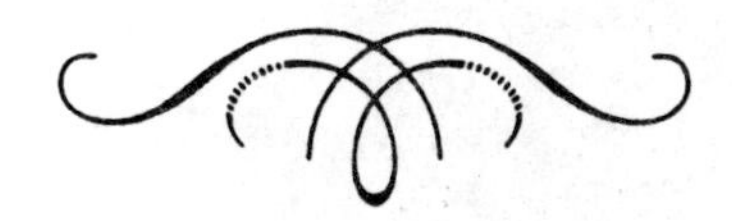

CHAPTER

3

Charley's 'Finds'.
The face at the window.
Sammy gets a ducking.

'It was a song thrush's nest all lined with mud and I thought the mother bird wouldn't mind if I only took one'.

There were baby stoats down by the willows near Slade Brook.

Slowly winter gave way to Spring.

March came with its blustery winds wild and showery and ragged clouds scudded across the sky, but the days began to get longer and a little warmer.

Martha Greenwood had told the children she would always be glad of some firewood and that she would pay them for whatever they brought. So they had found another way to earn a little money. They collected faggots from the spinneys round about and tying it in bundles, sold it, not only to Martha but to other villagers as well. Charley could also help with this, which pleased Beth for it kept him busy and out of mischief. Sometimes they all went together, sometimes the boys by themselves. Charley was in his element. He loved wandering about the woods and commons and 'finding things' as he said.

One day he came back panting, cheeks glowing and burst into the house where Beth was preparing the meal.

'Beth, what did I find today?' he cried.

'A hedgehog.'

'No, how silly thou art – they're still asleep.'

'I can't guess – tell me.'

Charley whisked his cap from behind. It was filled with grass and in the middle lay a beautiful green-blue egg spattered with reddish-brown spots and blotches.

'Charley!' Beth remonstrated, 'that would have been a baby bird!'

'But there were four more eggs in the nest. It was a thrush's,' he went on eagerly. 'It looked just like a ball of hay and twigs and it was on the top of a hawthorn tree.'

'So you threw your cap in the air, you were so excited and it fell down in the mud and then you climbed up to see and got all scratched and dirty.'

'How did thee know?' Charley was amazed.

'Because I have eyes to see and because I know thee. Thy clothes take twice as much washing and mending as John's and mine put together.'

'But it was worth it Beth – it was a song thrush's, all lined with mud and I thought the mother bird wouldn't mind if I only took one.'

Another day he came back, just as dirty and just as excited – he had seen some baby stoats down by the willows near Slade

Brook. 'There were six or seven,' he said breathlessly, 'and they were playing with a dead rabbit, but when they saw me they ran off up an old willow tree that was hollow in the middle. There were some holes in the trunk and I'm sure I could see their black eyes looking at me. They'd left the rabbit lying on the grass – I expect they'd come back when I'd gone and take it to their house inside the tree.'

'Just as long as Stoats or weasels or birds or snails or whatever else thee collects do not find their way into our house, I don't mind,' laughed Beth, for she had found weird things from time to time, even in the bedroom.

One day they went to Bluebell Wood which was not far from their cottage. They did not always stay together and on this particular day the boys had wandered off looking for more broken branches and left Beth tying up what they had already collected. She had finished some of the bundles but had quite a few more to do, when she fancied she heard footsteps on the woodland path. Thinking it was John or Charley returning, she called out to them but no one answered.

The footsteps had stopped but she thought she heard a twig snap and a slight rustling among the hazel boughs. Somewhat alarmed she looked all round but told herself she had probably imagined the footsteps. 'It's most likely a bird or woodland animal,' she thought to herself and in fact, at that moment, a pigeon began cooing in a nearby tree.

A few minutes later John and Charley appeared laden with more wood for her to tie. She said nothing to them for they would probably have laughed at her fears, but as they went off again, she stood for some seconds listening and looking at the thicket. Once more she was sure there was a slight rustling of the branches, and as she gazed, there were two eyes not many paces from her.

Like a startled deer she dropped the wood and leaving it all on the ground, fled as swiftly as her feet would carry her, out of the wood, on to the road and back to their cottage.

Almost an hour passed and the boys had not returned. She opened the door a little way and peeped out to see if they were coming.

To her amazement, there in front of her, was all the kindling she had tied up, and all she was going to tie. Here was a mystery indeed. She always knew there were fairy folk about in the woods – could it be they had spirited the fire wood to her door? John and Charley came soon after. Seeing the bundles they were very surprised that Beth had managed to get it all home by herself, but when they heard the story, they were just as puzzled as she was.

That was not the end of the mystery however, for the next morning when John went outside to pick up their buckets and get water from the well, they were already full and standing by the door. Charley stared at them awestruck. 'It must be the fairy folk!' he said.

When the boys put the wood on to their hand-cart and went off to sell it, Beth made sure she shut and fastened the door securely before she got out her mending. (Charley had been careless again). She had been sitting quietly for ten minutes or so when she heard some stealthy footsteps approaching the door.

They stopped, and Beth sat as still as a mouse, biting her nail and holding her breath. Perhaps it was someone coming to visit her, but why did they not knock at the door? Someone or something was standing close to it, listening.

The steps seemed to move cautiously. There was another pause. Beth did not stir but looked towards the window. Slowly the top of a head rose up against the panes with a crown on it, a green crown studded with gold, followed by a face. When Beth got over her fright and amazement she realised the face belonged to no one more fearful than Sammy Greenwood. She flung open the door and thrust back the red-gold hair that blew over her eyes.

'Sammy!' she cried. 'What on earth's thee doing there?' Sammy grinned all over his face and jumped from one foot to the other as he pointed to a pile of wood. His 'crown' made of ivy leaves decorated with coltsfoot and and daisy chains, sat crookedly on his straw-coloured hat; long, dangling hazel catkins dancing as he jumped to and fro. 'Thank thee Sammy,' said Beth giving him a friendly pat. 'Thou art a good lad. I'll find thee an apple from the barrel.' Still hopping from one foot to the other, Sammy pointed to the pile of wood.

'More? More?' he shouted.

'No more Sammy – thank thee no more today. Now thou must go home. Thy mother will think thou art lost and be worried,' and she pointed across to Underwood Common.

Sammy grinned all over his face and jumped from one foot to the other as he pointed to the pile of wood.
'More? More?' he shouted.

Sammy understood and nodded, again shaking his 'crown' awry and making the swinging catkins dance as he loped away across West Meadow.

Beth had heard strange sounds before outside the house but had dismissed them from her mind as being the usual country noises. Now everything was plain. The poor harmless lad had been hanging around their cottage for days wanting to show how grateful he was for their kindness to him. Beth wondered if Mistress Greenwood knew about it and decided to go and see her.

'Sammy likes to wander off and I do not worry too much unless he is away a long time,' she said. 'I did not know of the wood and water but in his own way he is always talking about you and it would make him very happy to do some small tasks. He is loving and docile,' she continued, 'to those who treat him kindly.'

So it was understood that Sammy came to their cottage from time to time and made himself busy by doing odd jobs for them. He loved apples but even when the barrel was empty, a nod and a smile from Beth, and he was amply repaid.

Beth in her turn had reason to be grateful to Mistress Greenwood (who insisted she should call her Martha). She was a thrifty and capable housewife, clever with her needle and spinning wheel and she helped Beth in many ways, for she could make a penny go farther than most. Although their ages were well apart, a strong bond of affection grew up between them.

From time to time she told Beth what herbs to find to make her cooking more tasty and gave her roots and seeds from her own garden. She told her what to collect for medicines and herb drinks – Coltsfoot for coughs, eye-bright and fennel for sore throats. Unlike most people at this time, Martha liked her house to be clean and sweet-smelling and always kept fresh rushes and lavender on her floor.

She was a good cook and gave Beth recipes for gingerbread and apple fritters, a favourite with the boys. One they loved especially was Savoury Pottage, using mutton, some oatmeal, parsley, sorrel, violet leaves, sweet marjoram and thyme. It had to be cooked over-night, left to stand and then boiled up next day.

Martha grew lots of plants and herbs round her neat little cottage up on Underwood Common.

April came, and in the woods wild primroses and violets hid shyly under their rosettes of leaves and the white tails of conies bobbed into their holes. Golden catkins swung on the hazels and starry white flowers spotted the blackthorn bushes. Mists hung over Slade Brook in the early mornings until the warming sun wisped them away and many an April shower brought out the good smells of the Spring earth.

The almost human cry of baby lambs was heard in Farmer Thacker's West Meadow. The first cuckoo called away in the woods and Charley came home with more 'finds' – one day it was frog or newt spawn, another, some baby mice no bigger than the joint of his thumb and still with their eyes shut. Beth put up with snails, beatles, caterpillars and even worms but she drew the line at mice.

'We should soon have the house awash with them,' she said aghast. Poor Beth, trying her hardest to copy Martha's cleanliness, was at her wit's end.

'What will thee bring home next?' she said in despair. 'Here take the basket and collect something useful – get some old fir cones – they make good kindling for the fire. There are plenty in the woods.'

Charley slung the basket of plaited reeds on his back and started off down to Slade Brook. Crossing over a shallow part on some large stepping stones, he was aware of being followed. A sidelong glance told him it was Sammy. Although he was still rather cautious of young Charley, (for the mischievous rascal would often play tricks on him) he would follow him about like a devoted dog. Charley for his part loved being in the woods, but liked it best with a companion – even if it was only Sammy.

On this particular day, having reached the other side of the brook, he put down the basket and turned round. 'You can come with me Sammy if you are my slave and carry the basket.'

Sammy did not understand what a slave was but nodded his head and he, trotting behind, they walked on.

Presently they came to a spot where cones lay thick on the ground under a group of fir trees. Charley pointed to the cones and the basket and while Sammy hopped about doing all the work, he seated himself on the moss-covered root of a tree and with an old rusty knife he always carried, began to make a whistle from a hollow stalk and after that, a bow and arrow - one of his favourite occupations.

Sammy worked on, not pausing till he saw Charley eating an apple, (he had found one last one at the bottom of the barrel) and then he stopped and looked at him, his mouth shutting and opening in time to Charley's bites. Chewing away with obvious enjoyment, Charley pointed to the partly filled basket and reluctantly Sammy returned to his gathering, still looking longingly at the apple. The core was eventually tossed into the basket where Sammy dived for it while Charley made weird noises on the whistle. But this was too tame for him. He was looking for more excitement than that and his active mind set about thinking of something to do.

As they sat by the side of the river, the rush basket between them, he had an idea. Jumping up, he seized Sammy's round cap with its cock feathers, and flung it with all his might into the high branches of an old alder tree. Fir cones scattered far and wide as Sammy leaped in the air, clapped his hands to his head and let out a loud howl. Charley prodded him with a stick.

'Go on Sam, get it!'

He knew Sammy could climb trees like a monkey and thought he would have some fun pelting him with cones and shooting at him with his bow and arrows.

Sammy started to climb, hampered somewhat by his long smock, stopping now and again to look at the cap still a good way above him. Presently he came to the branch where it had lodged, a branch that hung well out over the water and, simple as he was, he had enough sense to know he must edge carefully along it.

He was almost there to the shouts of, 'Go on Sammy!' from below, when suddenly something struck his leg. It was one of Charley's arrows. Sammy was not hurt but surprised, and instinctively put his hand to the spot.

He wobbled as he lost his balance and howling and frantically grabbing at small branches which broke in his fingers, he fell headlong with a tremendous splash into the water which was quite deep in this part of the brook.

Charley gasped in horror. What should he do? He could not swim and he was quite sure Sammy could not either. He would be blamed he knew that.

Suddenly something struck his leg. It was one of Charley's arrows. He wobbled as he lost his balance, and, howling and frantically grabbing at small branches, he fell headlong with a tremendous splash into the water.

'I'll run off,' he thought, 'Sammy's always wandering about the woods – he could easily have slipped in the water.'

No, he could not do that.

Sammy's unearthly screams, howls and gasps and the threshing of the water told him he had no time to lose. He must find a long branch that he could throw in and hope Sammy would grab hold of it.

In his terror he had not heard running footsteps along the river bank and as he jumped round, he came face to face with John. Beth, thinking he had been gone a long time and might perhaps need some help, had sent John to look for him. Yells and screams led to the spot. Flinging off his doublet and shirt he jumped in and brought Sammy, struggling, gasping and spluttering, to the bank, where he pushed and Charley pulled till he was on dry land again. He was shivering and whimpering as water dripped from his clothes and ran down into his shoes.

All they could do was to run back to the cottage where Beth did her best to dry them out before John saw Sammy safely home. All the way there, he was trying to tell him something and would keep banging his hands to his head.

All John could tell Martha was, where he found him and that he seemed to have lost his cap. Again she was very grateful that John had been there to save him. 'My poor boy. Never mind about the cap. I have another one,' she said as Sammy still persisted in uttering unintelligible sounds and banging his head with his hands.

At home Charley kept very quiet and Beth suspected the worst. 'However did Sammy come to be in the water? Was he with you?

'Yes, we had been collecting the fir cones and walking along the river bank and he fell in. I couldn't help it.'

Beth looked at him hard and straight. 'I hope thou art telling me the truth,' she said. 'The hobgoblins get those who tell lies.'

'I hope thou art telling me the truth,' she said.
'The hobgoblins get those who tell lies.'

CHAPTER

4

Beth and the Witch of Slade Wood

Primroses and violets looked up shyly from their hiding places, and blue harebells shook their heads and laughed.

It was a sunny afternoon in April and Beth had gone for some bread to the village bakery on Market Hill.

Suddenly an old woman on the opposite side of the street stumbled with a cry of pain, her crutch and stout walking stick making a clatter as she fell on the rough cobbles. To Beth's amazement the two or three folk nearby, edged away into a whispering group.

She ran across, helped the old woman to her feet and picked up the sticks. Her black steeple hat lay in the mud and her grey hair hung raggedly under her coif. A small crowd had gathered now, but at a distance, and heads together, they were muttering to each other. Then one detached herself from the others and beckoning to Beth, made urgent signs for her to come away. She heard the words 'witch' and 'Devil' and 'Black Magic'. Then she realised that this poor soul, who looked for all the world like a sack of old clothes, was the woman the villagers called the 'Witch'. She had heard of her and knew she lived in an isolated cottage in the middle of Slade Wood, but she had never seen her before.

She looked from the crowd to the old woman, who, still dazed from her fall, had picked up her steeple hat and put it drunkenly on her head. Her long nose and pointed chin almost met as she muttered some unintelligible words. The crowd edged nearer.

'Don't you know it's Joanne Stephens!' cried one. 'She's a witch!'

'Leave her alone – she'll fly home on her crutch!'

There was a roar of laughter.

'The hag'll put a spell on yer and yer family.'

'Aye, she looked at my pig and it died!'

They all nodded their heads.

'She never buys any food – she eats new-born babies!'

'She's got a black cat an' what's that if it ain't the sign of a witch?' shouted one looking round at the nodding group.

'And a goat!' shouted another, *He's* the Devil in disguise!'

'She only pretended to fall so she could get you in her clutches!'

Beth looked toward them, half afraid, but she was her father's daughter and did not lack courage and now some words of his came back to her – 'Good is always stronger than evil.' Besides she had some rosemary and lavender in her pocket and they were sure safeguards against black magic and the evil eye. She looked at the old woman again and saw only a poor old soul in need.

'Come,' she said kindly, 'I'll help you home.'

The crowd by the Market House were still shouting.

'It's the Ponder wench – perhaps she's a witch too!'

Beth grasped her loaf and the stick and put the wrinkled old hand round her shoulder, helping her along as she hobbled with the crutch under the other arm. They took a short cut through the Church Yard to Kettering Road and then on down the hill, oh, so slowly it seemed to Beth, for the old woman had hurt her leg in the fall. Half-way down they came to Meadow Lane.

'If thou art all right,' said Beth, 'I'll take this bread home and be back in a minute.'

The old crone nodded and Beth dashed off. It felt good to be running.

Home was familiar and safe. Should she bolt the door and stay there? If she *was* a witch she could work her magic and get back by herself. No – she could not leave her, but it was with some reluctance she joined the old woman on Kettering Road again.

She stood where she had left her, leaning heavily on her crutch and stick. 'You are very kind my dear,' she said as they resumed the slow, painful progress down to the bridge that humped over Slade Brook. Here they turned off the road along a rough brookside path where the going was hard. Presently they left this also and went along a track that led deep into the wood.

The sun was getting low in the West and sending shafts of light through the thinner branches, but the foliage now made it seem darker and it was difficult to walk side by side for the path was narrow and Beth was constantly trying to brush away the branches and hazel twigs that hit their faces.

Then, all at once, in a small clearing, there it was, the 'Witch's Cottage', built with rough wooden planks and thatched with rushes, more like a woodman's hut than a cottage, Beth thought.

Sure enough on a patch of moss and grass, a goat was tethered. Beth looked half fearfully. *Was* it the Devil in dis-

Beth did her best to help the old 'witch' home.

The 'Witch's Cottage' was built with rough wooden planks and thatched with rushes

guise? And by the door sat a black cat. Its bright green eyes shone in the half light. She felt for the rosemary and lavender again in her pocket.

The old woman pushed open the door with her stick. It was quite dark inside for the only window was very small and covered with oiled paper. An acrid smell of wood smoke hung round the room. 'Come in my dear, if you will and light the dip for me – the tinder box is somewhere.' She clutched hold of the rough wooden table as she shuffled round it to a stool.

Beth could not find the box but there was a glimmer on the hearth stone and some kindling lying by so she managed to coax the dying embers into a little flame and from it lit the home-made rush light. This only seemed to deepen the darkness of the strange little room – the only room as far as Beth could see. A draught from the door or wall chinks sent the flame dipping and showed a bed of rags on the floor with a straw-filled pillow. Smoke hung round the room in a haze and made her eyes smart. The black cat rubbed round her legs purring, its tail straight up in the air.

'If thou are all right now Mistress Stephens, I'll be getting home,' said Beth, 'but I'll come tomorrow if you like, to see if you want anything.'

'Thank ye kindly my dear, – away ye get now afore it grows too dark.' Beth closed the door with a certain relief.

It was not difficult to see under the trees, for a pale silver moon had risen and got tangled with the branches, but it was eerie there by herself. A breeze had sprung up and to Beth it seemed as if the trees were whispering together and waving witch-like arms to catch her.

A twig snapped behind her. She jumped quickly to face it. Was there a hobgoblin or foul fiend behind that dark tree? An owl hooted. She felt her goose pimples rise and ran the last few yards to the brook path, catching her breath as though the Devil himself was at her heels.

Here; away from the trees it was lighter. There was a plop in the water as she ran along – probably a fish or moorhen. A few yards farther – and then, oh, how good it was to be safely on Kettering Road again and not far from home.

Her sleep that night was disturbed by strange dreams but she had put some fennel in the keyhole to keep evil away and in the morning they were all still safe and well, John and

Charley with their usual healthy appetites.

So, true to her word she went back to the witch's cottage carrying a bit of their rabbit, stewed with herbs and vegetables, in a basin.

It was a different wood from the evening before. Sunlight and shadow dappled the mossy floor, primroses and violets looked up shyly from their hiding places, blue harebells shook their heads and laughed and golden catkins danced on the hazel bushes. As she got to the cottage door she noticed a broomstick by the wall – a broomstick – witches had broomsticks – but when she looked at it closely, it looked no different from her own besom at home.

The old woman was sitting where she had left her the night before. Beth wondered if she had even been to bed. 'Good morrow Mistress Stephens!' Beth greeted her cheerily.

'It's kind of you to come my dear.'

She saw Beth looking at the table. 'I was just mixing myself a potion,' she said.

Powdered eggshells, some snails, seeds and hips and haws burned to blackness, were being pestled together in a basin with water, soap and honey, and in a skillet on the fire was what smelled like a poisonous brew of herbs.

'This will do me a lot of good,' she said, tasting and giving it a stir.

Beth had been clutching the basin of rabbit stew and now held it out to her. The smell was appetizing and she seemed pleased with it.

'You're a good girl,' she said softly, looking piercingly at her through her kindly old eyes. 'You'll have some sorrow but you'll have some joy. Before long a tall dark man will come into your life who will be a very good friend to you. He will be wearing a long black cloak and a sugar-loaf hat.'

'Sounds like my father,' Beth smiled.

'No not him.' The old crone shook her head.

'I'll collect some sticks for thy fire while I am here and fetch thee some water,' and she picked up a basket of plaited rushes and an old wooden bucket from behind the door.

Sticks lay everywhere under the trees so that filling did not take long, and it only seemed a step or two to the stream for the water.

When she got back the rabbit stew had been put into the

skillet and Mistress Stephens handed her the basin. In it was a small packet of something fastened up in dirty oiled skin.

'I have no money to pay you my dear,' she said, 'but keep very safely what is in that packet. Do not open it unless you are in dire need and if so take it to Doctor Cogan at his apothecary's shop. He will know what to do with it.'

Beth was puzzled but thanked her and waved as the old woman came to see her off.

'Three things to remember my dear, don't cross bridges before you come to them, look after today and tomorrow will look after itself, and, it's always the darkest hour before the dawn.'

'What queer things to say,' thought Beth as she walked back through the wood and along by the river, in full spate after the Spring rains and gurgling merrily.

'How could you cross a bridge before you came to it? And how could tomorrow look after itself? The darkest hour before the dawn?' That puzzled her still more.

There was a 'bridge to cross' however, as soon as she got home. John had fetched the 'Hidey' Box and was counting its contents. 'We've hardly any money left,' he said. 'I'm going to Farmer Thacker to see if I can help with the haymaking and perhaps later with the harvest. It will be little enough he pays me, but 'twill help. We have spent more on food than I thought. We must try to take none out for a while or there will not be enough when Bailiff Foggarty comes in June.'

Beth nodded and wrinkled her brow. She did wish there was something *she* could do. This thought occupied her mind as she was busy with her household tasks.

'Father said God would supply all our needs but how He can do that I don't know,' she pondered doubtfully. She had forgotten about the packet the witch had given her until she saw it on the three-legged stool.

'She told me to keep it safely and only to open it if we were in dire trouble. Now where can I put it? I know – the Hidey Box!' Yes, the money in there *was* getting very low.

Again she tried to think of something she could do.

She felt happier when John came back looking pleased and excited. 'Farmer Thacker says he may have a job for me,' he had been running and was out of breath. 'He's not hay cutting yet, but says I can help with jobs around the farm.'

'What will he pay thee?'

'The usual I expect – three pence a day with some food at the farm or seven pence if I come home. Cheer up Beth, eighteen pence a week will buy us some mutton, bread, eggs and milk and he will probably keep me on till Michaelmas to help with the harvest if I give satisfaction – and what's more our Charley can have a job scaring birds off his crops along the Kettering Road. He'll have to go very early in the mornings and he'll pay him a halfpenny a day.'

Beth was pleased, especially about Charley's little job. He was getting quite a handful sometimes and that would keep him out of mischief she hoped. She still wished *she* could have a job too.

'I know,' she thought, 'women haymakers get two pence a day for tossing the cut grass over with forks. I wonder if Farmer Thacker would employ me too?'

When she went to see him however, he shook his head and said he had enough village women already. She was disappointed but Beth was always an optimist.

'Something may turn up, we'll manage somehow,' she thought to herself. 'We've got some food for today at any rate,' and suddenly the old witch's words came back to her

'Tomorrow will look after itself.'

'I have no money to pay you my dear, but keep very safely what is in this packet. Do not open it unless you are in dire need and if so take it to Doctor Cogan at his apothecary's shop.'

CHAPTER 5

Charley learns to write.
Martha goes to Northampton.
A visit from 'Watercress' Willy.

'Give you good day lady – any ribbons or laces, chin clouts or buskins!'
'Why, Watercress Willy!' Beth laughed.

Charley had worried her a good deal lately little scallywag that he was. She was sure he could be good at learning if he would only try. Their father had taught both John and Beth to read and write and now she was trying her hardest to teach Charley. He was not a very willing pupil and escaped whenever he could but she was determined that at any rate he should be able to write his name.

So one morning during the next week he was caught and made to sit down at the table. She had found a piece of wood and some charcoal from the fire.

'Come on,' she said, 'C – that is the first letter of Charley. I'll write them all and then you can copy them.' Charley hooked his ankles round the legs of the stool and whistled one of his tuneless ditties.

'For goodness sake stop whistling Charley, it sounds like the wind in the chimney.'

He clutched the charcoal in his hand, his tongue making circles round and round as he struggled with the C. He rubbed it out several times till Beth was satisfied, and then went to H, his neck stretching and his chin pulled down. A seemed to need two commanding strokes and he pulled up his drooping shoulders like a soldier and pressed hard. Then came R, L, and E which he wrote backwards. Scratching the charcoal down the board, and with white knuckles struggling and his feet swinging back and forth, he finished off the Y.

Just at this juncture there was a knock at the door and in came Martha and Sammy, the latter clapping his hands and hopping from one foot to the other, a new cap on his head stuck with feathers.

'I have some good news for you,' smiled Martha. 'You know I have been working at the Manor House recently for Sir Aldwig DuVayne, helping out at busy times. Beth nodded. Charley had escaped out of the door.

'Well, they asked me yesterday if I knew of a young girl to work in the kitchen – washing up – doing vegetables – things like that, and I immediately thought of you. You would get two pence a day and some food there.'

Beth was delighted. 'When can I start?' she asked.

'Go to the kitchen door tomorrow and tell them I sent you.'

'Won't *you* be going?'

'Not tomorrow nor for some time to come I fear. I have told you of my brother who lives in Northampton.' Beth nodded.

His wife is sick and he wants me to go and look after her and the children for a while.'

'How long wilt thou be away?'

'I cannot tell, till my sister-in-law is better I expect.'

Beth's face fell. She had come to have a great affection for Martha and to rely on her help and encouragement. Besides, part of her pleasure in working at the Manor would be that Martha was there as well. She was very quiet as she moved over to the fire, raked the embers and stirred the contents of the iron pot which hung there. Martha saw her disappointment and put a motherly arm about her shoulders.

'Cheer up Beth, see what I've brought you!' It was some of her famous gingerbread.

'I shall not be away for ever. I'm not looking forward to going either,' she continued, 'but it is my duty to help if I can; and there is one good thing about this, I may be able to visit your father and perhaps take him a little something from time to time.' Beth's face brightened. As she flung her arms round Martha there were tears in her eyes but a smile also.

'Thou art the kindest soul on earth,' she said.

Charley said he would never *be able to write.*

Martha had to go, for she and Sammy were to catch the stage wagon when it stopped at the Crown Inn. Beth walked with them up Kettering Road as far as Squire's Hill to the inn yard, Martha in a scarlet cloak over her grey kirtle and a straw hat tied over her white coif.

Presently the stage wagon with its broad wheels lumbered noisily into the cobbled yard. Some passengers alighted, ostlers hurried to its four horses and changed them for fresh ones, the Rowell travellers got in, the coachman (having finished his tankard of ale) climbed onto the front horse, and with a whip, a shout and a cry they were off again.

Beth watched till the covered wagon was out of sight and then made her way back home again with a heavy heart. Neither John nor Charley were there and the house seemed dull and empty.

Suddenly there was a shrill whistling outside and a 'Rat-a-tat' on the door. Beth opened it.

'Give you good day lady, any ribbons or laces, chin clouts or buskins, buttons or bows, scissors or combs, inkle, pouches or sticken pins?'

'Why, Watercress Willy!' she laughed, 'It's good to see thee again – it must be a twelvemonth since you last called!'

Although he was known everywhere as 'Watercress Willy', Willy Lott was a pedlar and always welcome in a village like Rowell with his great pack of goods on his back and his tray of trinkets in front.

Willy was born at Naseby, seven miles as the crow flies from Rowell, and from a young boy he had gathered anything the countryside had to offer, herbs, nuts, berries, mushrooms, watercress, (hence his name) and peddled them at all the markets. He had been very poor in those early days and more than once Nathaniel Ponder had cobbled up a pair of old shoes for him, always refusing to take any money for them. Beth was pleased when he came, for it often meant material for a new kirtle, a capa or a pinner.

'Come in Willy, thou art welcome – I see thou art well.' And then she added sadly, 'I fear there is nothing I can buy from thee this time. Our father has been put in Northampton Gaol for preaching and 'tis a hard job we have to get enough to eat.' Willy came in, his black hair curling under his broad-brimmed hat.

' 'Tis good to see you again young Mistress Beth – why how you have grown since I saw you last – how you *have grown*.' And he looked her up and down. He had a crooked back from always carrying a heavy load and a one-sided smile to go with it.

'Thee can have a bite to eat Willy if thee likes, but 'tis only herbs and vegetables in the pot thickened with oatmeal.' He thanked her, unloaded the great pack from his back and took off the tray he carried in front as she put down a wooden platter and spoon before him and ladled out the gallimaufry. He ate it with obvious relish, his tongue circling his lips to grab any loose bits and grinned up at Beth, his eyes making slits in his weather-beaten face and his black curly locks still wet with perspiration.

'Ah, something I meant to ask you,' Willy stopped, food halfway to his mouth.

'What has happened to Mother Stephens?'

'The one they call the witch? I know of nothing. I saw her but a few days past. Why?'

'As I came by her cottage – where she has mixed me many a potion over the years for the colic or the ague or to cure my warts – it wasn't there any more.'

Beth stopped half-way to the fire. 'Not there?'

'Nothing left but a heap of ashes with her old iron pot in the middle of them lying on its side.'

'And Mistress Stephens – and her cat and goat?'

'Not a sign anywhere. I shouted and called for a good ten minutes but only the echo of my own voice came back through the trees.'

'They called her a witch in Rowell,' Beth mused and recalled how the crowd shouted at her when she fell in the Market Square. She also remembered hearing a noisy mob passing two nights ago but had thought they were returning from Kettering with, as John said, 'too much ale in their bellies'.

'Poor Joanne Stephens. That was her little home. I wonder where she has gone?'

'Ever heard of swimming a witch"?' Willy looked up at her from under his eyes.

Beth nodded. She knew what he meant. She pictured the poor old soul thrown into Slade Brook. If she sank, she was innocent. If she managed to scramble out – guilty.

'She knew a lot of things, perhaps she managed to get away before they came.'

Willy shook his head sadly. 'I doubt if we will ever know. She was just a poor old woman – but a very wise one.'

Just at this moment, Charley, (whose stomach always told him when it was time to eat) burst in at the door with John close behind him. 'Watercress Willy!' they cried together.

They too always enjoyed his visits, not so much for all the exciting things he carried, as for the exciting stories he told of his travels far and wide.

'What's to do in the great world Willy?' asked John.

'Well, you've heard about the King by now of course.'

John nodded. 'Aye, about his execution in London Town.'

'The thirtieth of January it was, and 1649 will be remembered in history for many a long year. I was there in the crowd.'

'You were there?' They all gathered closer.

'Aye 'twas a bitter cold morning, by my troth, and snowing. A staging had been put up outside the royal palace in Whitehall. A great crowd had gathered and there was a mighty noise, but all fell silent when the King stepped out from a window.'

'What was he like?' Charley was as near to Willy as he could get.

'He was tall and moved very nobly, like a hero, toward a block of wood, where a great brawny man stood holding an axe, his face partly covered by a black mask. The King said something to Bishop Juxton who stood beside him and he bowed his head and nodded.'

'What happened then?' Charley's mouth and eyes were open wide.

'He knelt down very slowly, his hands together as if he was saying a prayer, like this,' and Willy acted it out very solemnly on the floor.

'There was a deadly silence in that vast throng of people as he laid his head on the block – it was just as though he was going to sleep. Then he suddenly stretched out his arms as a signal to the axeman. A great gasp went through the crowd as the axe did its deadly work, and as the executioner held up the fallen head, and shouted, "Behold the head of a traitor!" A loud groan arose from the multitude.'

Beth screwed her eyes and hands together.

'It was the Naseby battle that was one of his great defeats at the hands of Cromwell and the Parliament men, and 'twas Cromwell who had him put to death. Some said he was a bad king but he looked kind of noble and gentle and sad to me – and Cromwell – well he's one of your Puritans isn't he? At any rate they say he prays a lot. I'm only a poor country pedlar and know naught of politics and governments – who's right or who's wrong, but it seemed a great shame to me, and they say he has a wife – and children. But now this Cromwell's in power he will for sure be passing laws in the Parliament House to get men like thy father out o'gaol.'

Beth's eyes were shining. 'Dost thou think so Willy?'

'Aye, indeed I do.'

'Tell us some more tales about the Battle of Naseby,' begged Charley, 'about Prince Rupert and how dashing and brave he was.'

'You've heard my Naseby battle stories before,' laughed Willy, 'and I must be on my way – but did I tell you about my two year old nephew Jamie?'

'No.' They shook their heads.

'Well, he was wandering along the village street, as you know little ones will, when some of Cromwell's troopers

Very solemnly Willy got down on the floor and acted out the King's execution.

came galloping through. He would surely have been trampled to death, but the leader stooped in his saddle, caught him by the nape of his neck and flung him over the churchyard wall. He fell on soft ground and was uninjured.'

'What a blessing that was!' Beth breathed.

'Ah, there's lots more I could tell you but I must be to Harborough by nightfall. Come little Beth, choose theeself some material for a kirtle in payment for the meal and for the kindness your father has always shown me – life's not about battles and kings but about helping each other.'

Willy unrolled his pack. There was a bewildering array of broadcloth and buriat, camlet made of goat's hair, coarse dowlas for shirts and aprons, woollen frieze for jerkins, doublets and gowns, durrance for petticoats, red stemmel cloth, and lindsey-woolsey with its silky finish. Willy held out some blue and scarlet duffel but Beth shook her head.

'Father will only let me wear a sober colour,' and she chose grey kersey, a coarse woollen cloth she thought would wear well and be warm for Winter.

'And there's thread to stitch it with and maybe for some mending,' said Willy, rummaging among the many articles in his tray. 'A stitch in time saves nine as my poor old mother used to say.'

'Thank you indeed Willy,' said Beth, 'Thou art very kind.'

'I wish I could travel with thee,' said Charley wistfully. Willy looked at him.

'Thee'll travel a lot farther than ever I have, when thee'st a man. Can you read and write yet?'

'I can write my name,' Charley replied, 'it's the same as the King's was, isn't it?'

'He's trying,' said Beth and she held up the piece of wood.

'That's a good lad – my mother – God rest her soul – tried to learn me once, but she gave it up poor woman and said, "you can't make a silk purse out of a sow's ear",' and he gave his one-sided grin. 'But I've done very well without it,' he mused, 'very well without it.' He finished packing his goods.

'Look after your sister Master John.' He hitched the great pack on to his back, set his tray to rights and was off, whistling as he went.

'God be wi' thee Watercress Willy!' they shouted after him.

'And with you!' he called back.

All that evening Beth could not help thinking about 'Mother Stephens' as Willy had called her. She did hope that, sensing trouble, she had gone away or hidden herself somewhere. She peered out into the starlit night and then before she climbed the stair to bed, put fennel in the keyhole as a precaution against all evil.

How long she had slept she could not tell, but she heard music and opening her eyes the room was filled with a soft, shimmering light and there was the old witch – no, it could not be her for she was dressed in golden robes with a jewelled crown on her head, not a steeple hat – and yet it *was* her for she recognised the kind eyes and the soft voice when she spoke.

'I want to give you a gift for your kindness to me,' she said. 'I could give you great wealth and riches beyond all dreams, but that would not make you happy, so I have decided to give you the gift of making everyone else happy where ever you go.'

The soft golden light suffusing the room seemed to grow brighter, and Beth woke with a start. The moonlight was flooding in through the tiny window right on to her face.

'What a strange dream – but a nice one,' she smiled as she turned over and went to sleep again.

She was dressed in golden robes
with a jewelled crown on her head.

CHAPTER

6

They all go to work:
Charley bird scaring: Beth to the Manor House:
John to Farmer Thacker's

'Them plaguey birds!' cried Charley and roared into battle again.

A cock crowed somewhere out in the darkness of a mid-April morning.

'Wake up Charley! – Charley, come on, bestir thyself, 'tis time we were off.' John was standing by the bed shaking him. Charley half woke and rolled over, burying his head in the bedcover.

' 'Tis still dark,' he grumled and rubbed his eyes sleepily.

'Come on, get up, thou hast to be scaring the crows by daybreak.'

Charley had been excited at the thought of earning a half penny a day, of being free and out of doors, but it was not quite so exciting to start off on a cold April morning with the stars still out.

John was going with him as far as Farmer Thacker's field and Beth gave him a hug and stood by the cottage door to see them off. They were soon lost in the darkness as they trudged along the road half-way to Kettering to the enclosure where Charley had to guard the wheat crop from thieving birds.

When they arrived, he put his belongings by a tree, his food tied in a kerchief, an old skillet he could bang with a stick and a piece of red stammel tied to a branch, to wave as he ran. John left him reluctantly. He seemed so small there in the darkness, but all he said was, 'Right Charley? I'll be for getting back or I'll be late myself at Farmer Thacker's'

Charley was used to wandering about the woods and commons and loved it, though it was usually with one of his friends. It was different in the cold darkness of early morning, all alone. He felt suddenly frightened as he saw his brother turn and go. Leaving his belongings by the tree, he crept back along the road they had come, hiding when he could, behind a bush, far enough back from the unsuspecting John but keeping his starlit silhouette just in sight. He jumped as a slight noise scared him – was it one of those hobgoblins Beth said were in the woods or perhaps even the Devil himself? He felt his hair standing on end. By the time they reached the outskirts of Rowell again, dawn was breaking in the Eastern sky and not so frightened now, he turned and went slowly back again.

Charley loved birds and knew many of them by sight and sound. In the early morning sunlight he could hear a chorus of song, a wren, piercingly sweet, blackbirds, thrushes, willow warblers. In the distance, rooks were swirling round a group of high elms and before long he could hear their raucous voices calling, 'Maud! Maud!' as, shiny coated, they settled out across the field. There were sparrows too, fighting and chattering in the new-sprung corn. Charley got to work. Banging the skillet dangling round his neck with one hand and waving his red stammel flag with the other, he dashed around giving yells enough to awaken the dead. The birds rose in a cloud and blew away like leaves in Autumn. But Charley knew he must keep a watchful eye – they would be back.

In the meantime he picked the seed-heads of some early dandelions and blew them away to see what time it was. 'Puff! One o'clock. Puff! Two o'clock. Puff! Three o'clock – four,' till there was nothing left but the bare head. Then he picked white dead-nettles and for something to do, sucked the flowers to taste the tiny bit of sweetness at the bottom. Away in a distant copse he heard, 'Cuckoo! Cuckoo!' and wondered if he would ever had the good fortune to find a cuckoo's egg in, say, a sparrow's nest as he had once found a young cuckoo with the featherless baby sparrows dead on the ground below. Here came the birds once more homing in on the cornfield. A cloud of starlings, their wings a-quiver, their bodies black against the morning light, blue-black rooks and lapwings with their plaintive, 'Pee-wit, Pee-wit,' rose and scattered as Charley banged and roared into battle again.

The danger over for the time being, he spotted some cow-parsley and dandelions. There was a glint in his eyes as he gathered as many leaves as he could. Their rabbits would love them. He looked up at the sky.

'Them plaguey birds are there again. I suppose they're after their breakfast,' he mused, and so was he. Opening the kerchief, he tucked into some bread smeared with dripping. Everything was all right now. It was broad daylight and the sun was getting warm.

As he sat eating however, a breeze blew up driving dark clouds across the sky and there was a sudden downpour of rain. Charley sheltered as best he could under a hawthorn bush until a few minutes later the rain eased and a bright shaft of sunlight shot out from behind the black cloud. Everything glistened as though it was made of silver. He peered up to the sky and there spanning it was the many-coloured arch of a rainbow. It looked as though it ended on the other side of his field and he remembered in one of Beth's stories there was a crock of gold at the end of a rainbow. He bounded through the corn but even as he did so, the rain stopped, the sun shone out full and splendidly and the rainbow faded. So ended his hopes of a crock of gold.

'And I was almost there,' he said disappointedly to himself.

Meanwhile, back at home Beth and John had their own problems. It was John's first day at Farmer Thacker's and Beth's at the Manor House. They were both a little apprehensive.

It was still very early when John arrived at Three Chimney's Farm on Loddington Road, but a horse dealer was already there with the farmer, a mountain of a man with a big red nose and a wart on the end of it. He was wanting a good strong plough horse and was running his hand down its legs, thwacking its shanks and pulling open its mouth. John stood waiting, till having decided to buy it, the farmer turned to him.

'So you're young Ponder. Glad ter see you're on time – glad ter see it.' He looked him up and down as he would another horse and John wondered if he was going to feel *his* limbs or look at *his* teeth. 'Yer don't look o'er strong ter me young fellow – well yer's got ter earn yer money or else yer goes, do yer understand?' John nodded.

'All I ask is thee'll give me a fair trial sir.'

'Very well – Isaac!' he shouted to one of his farm hands. 'Take this lad with you into the yard and get it cleared.'

Isaac, a cocky youth of eighteen or so, with brawny arms and legs, who rather fancied himself in his thigh-length jerkin, his knee-breeches and sugar-loaf hat stuck with a jaunty feather, looked him up and down and then led the way to a yard enclosed by farm-buildings where cattle stood deep in dung-soaked straw, discoloured and dank. He adjusted his rolled up stockings and pulled the buckle of his jerkin tighter.

'Got ter clear this lot out and put fresh straw in,' was his terse remark. 'Back up the cart Joe!' he shouted to a fellow labourer, and to John, 'Get a hold o' a fork or spade and fill it bang up.'

It was black and heavy and very tiring this dung carting and it was soon evident to John that 'Master Isaac' intended him to do the bulk of the hard work. He managed sometimes to get a minute's rest between the dispatch of a full cart and the backing into position of an empty one. At one time, stretching his back for a rest, and wiping off the sweat with the sleeve of his shirt, he heard an unearthly squealing.

'What's that?' He looked startled.

'Oh that,' said Isaac, casually tipping back the sugar-loaf hat with its jaunty feather, 'they're killing a pig.' They went on working but John could not forget that pig's last agonising cry.

From time to time Farmer Thacker came to see why they were not yet finished. 'Yer a pair o' lazy louts!' he shouted. 'I could ha' done it meself in half the time – in half the time. If it ain't finished within the next half hour, there'll be nowt for either of thee at dinner time – nowt at all.'

Isaac took off his hat and gave a sweeping bow to the farmer's receding back.

Eventually the yard was cleared and fresh straw spread in. The cattle rustled among it, resting in its new cleanliness.

'Ha' ter be done again in a day or two,' was Isaac's comment as he chewed on a straw.

Farmer Thacker was a driver, he always made sure none of his farm hands were ever idle. The yard finished he sent them off to the fields where the dung had been dropped in heaps to be spread for next year's crop. Never had a morning seemed so long, John thought – but it was not finished yet.

Returning from the muck spreading, he and Isaac were set to work on a hand-mill grinding corn for Goodwife Thacker. 'The grain goes in this hopper at the top,' Isaac pointed out and then, one on each side of the mill, they turned a handle rotating two stone wheels until the flour fell into a sack at the bottom. It took a while and John began to wonder if he had any arms left and when the dinner would be brought to them. At any rate on this job, Isaac had to do his share.

At last out came two servant wenches with the victuals, one slyly shy as she looked at the farm lads from under her dark lashes, and the other, with apple-red cheeks and laughing eyes, giving them a chafing remark and a back kick with her heel as she passed. Isaac stood feet apart and arms akimbo, his hat with the feather at a jaunty angle, eyeing them with a twinkle

A servant wench, with apple-red cheeks and laughing eyes, came out with the victuals, giving the farm lads a chaffing remark and a back kick with her heel as she passed.

in his eye as they laid out a cloth on the floor and placed flagons of ale, bread and cheese, home cured ham and cold bread pudding, on it. Goodwife Thacker followed and seeing young Isaac ripe for mischief, bundled the two girls back into the house, 'Apple-cheeks', in her straw hat and laced bodice, bobbing out her tongue at him as she went.

Farm-hands, shepherds, dairymen, labourers all gathered round, some kneeling, some standing, to eat and drink.

'Come on lad.' It was old Tom who spoke – 'Hatchet' to his friends because of the shape of his face – a jolly soul, wrinkled by the suns and winds of seventy years. 'Get going boy, bit o' nice home-cured ham there.'

John looked. The shriek of the dying pig still rang in his ears. 'No thank ye,' he said. But the hard work had given him an appetite and he fell to with a will on the bread and cheese. 'Hatchet' devoured some cold bread pudding, holding it in his gnarled old hands, spat, and tipped down his beer without so much as a swallow.

'Come and sit in the sun boy, it's cold in the swaile,' he said, puffing at his upturned clay pipe.

'Ah, quick enough to eat me victuals I see young Ponder.' It was farmer Thacker. 'But don't take all day – don't take all day. There's some drainage trenches to be cut down Broad Meadow. Take the trenching plough and gouge Isaac and show him how to do it – how to do it.'

John knew what that meant. Young Isaac would do a small bit and then watch him do the rest. He had been at work since daybreak and by nightfall he ached in every limb and wondered if he had any strength left to drag himself home.

Beth and Charley were there before him, both with their tales to tell. He had a dip in the water bucket outside.

'Good old Beth,' he said coming in and throwing himself down on the floor rushes, for an appetising smell rose from the iron pot over the fire.

'Oh, poor John,' said Beth sympathetically, 'thou must have had a really hard day!'

'I shall have muscles of iron if I work at Farmer Thacker's for long,' John managed to laugh.

'Come and eat thy supper. I've such a lot to tell thee,' and she ladled out the mutton stew and placed rye bread and a brown earthenware pitcher of ale on the table. 'May the good

Lord be praised for this our daily bread – amen.' she said.
'Amen,' they echoed and then fell to.

Beth was longing to tell them about her day at the Manor, but she knew they would be better listeners on full stomachs so she bided her time and heard their stories first, Charley carefully omitting in his, the part where he followed John back almost into Rowell.

'That's my Charley,' said Beth, 'I knew thee'd do that job all right.'

And then she started. 'Oh John,' she said excitedly, 'You've never seen a house like it – I knew it was big, but BIG!' and she waved her arm wildly. 'It's bigger than all the cottages in Rowell put together. I went to the kitchen door as Martha had told me and said who I was. One they call Goodwife Vialls, looked me up and down, stuck her nose in the air and sniffed but cook and the other servants seemed friendly enough. Oh but the kitchen – it must be ten times bigger than our house. There was a huge fire with great spits roasting – yes roasting, half an ox and several chickens. There's big shiny copper pans and skillets and bowls and porringers and dishes and ladles and spoons, and candlesticks with real candles in them, and pitchers and flagons; and hanging up are sides of ham and bacon and all sorts of herbs and I don't know what else besides – and the floor was made of stone slabs not hardened mud like ours.' Beth had to pause for breath.

'I should think you spent your day just looking at the kitchen,' laughed John. 'Never mind what was *in* the kitchen, what came *out* of it?'

'You mean, what did the cook, cook?'

John and Charley looked at each other and nodded in unison.

'Well,' Beth went on, 'that too was exciting. Beside the meat and chickens I told thee of, there was a lovely smell of bread in the oven and the cook had made tarts and pies and venison pasties and gingerbread.'

She paused for breath.

'And who was going to eat all that food?' John wanted to know.

'Well, there's Sir Aldwig DuVayne, Lady Margaret, his wife, their three daughters, Abigail, Alianore and Joan.'

'But that's only five.'

'Oh John,' said Beth excitedly, 'you've never seen a house like it. I knew it was big, but BIG! – it's bigger than all the cottages in Rowell put together!'

'Maybe they were having some company, how would I know? Quite a lot came back to the kitchen though and all the servants had some.'

'Did you?'

'Oh yes, I had some venison pasty – that's made from deer's meat thee knowest. They want me to go for two weeks so that I can help when they have the great May Ball – that's sure to be a splendid affair.'

John looked at Beth's shining eyes, her cheeks flushed from the fire and the silky red-gold hair that fell about her face and shoulders from under her white coif.

'And what work did my sister have to do'?

'Washing up mostly, and that made my back ache bending over the stone sink and scouring the greasy skillets and dishes and plates and porringers. I had to carry hot water from a copper in what they called the scullery. That was hard work. Then I had to clean some vegetables, carrots, cabbages and onions and some yellowy things called potatoes. They grow all these in the kitchen garden and cook sent me out once to get more from one of the gardeners. I was glad – the sun was shining and it was good to be outside. As I ran along I met such a fine gentleman, I couldn't help staring at him. He was much taller than you John, with a cocked hat trimmed with feathers and ribbon loops and long curly hair and a lace cravat and a long coat and waistcoat all buttons and fancy braid and shoes with heels and big bows in front and – '

'Steady on old Beth, catch thy breath, he was a fine gentleman, leave it at that,' said John.

'He certainly was, and then I heard someone saying, 'Curtsey to Sir Aldwig.' It was one of the gardeners. I had no idea it was he, so I curtsied and dropped my head, I was ashamed of having stared so hard. I wanted to run off but he put his hand under my chin and lifted it up. 'And who have we here?' he said.

'Elizabeth Ponder an' it please you Sir,' I replied, and he said,

'It does please me. You're a pretty little wench. So you're Nathaniel Ponder's daughter?'

'Yes Sir,' I replied, and said I'd come to work in the kitchen.

Right" he said, then be off with you!" very fiercely, but I

don't think he was angry with me. I ran and hid till he had gone before I asked for the vegetables but when I got back to the kitchen I almost got a beating for being a long time.'

John sat by the embers for some while that night. He was troubled in his mind. Although Charley had said nothing, he knew he had been frightened left alone in the darkness. He wondered how long he himself could keep up the hard work at the farm, and last of all he was worried about Beth, worried because she was seeing a different sort of world from theirs. What would it do to her? Worried too that she almost got a beating. But they needed some money and he could see no other way out.

'I suppose we must be grateful,' he thought as he finally climbed the stair to bed, for before he knew it another day would be knocking at the door.

'And who have we here?' he said.
'Elizabeth Ponder an' it please you Sir.'
'It does please me. You're a pretty little wench.'

CHAPTER 7

'Woolly' comes to live with them.
Preparations at the Manor for the May Ball.
Lady Margaret's offer.
May Day – Beth meets Owen Ragford

Beth stood watching the Maypole dancers.
'Not joining in the fun?' asked Owen Ragford.
'No sir, my father says merrymaking and dancing are inventions of the Devil.'

The last fortnight in April was a busy one on the farm and John came home tired and hungry each evening. In some ways he was getting used to his work there and even enjoying it, especially when he could help round up the sheep and lambs, feed the pigs and their new families with milk and whey and offals from the farm kitchen, or watch the geese and ducklings doing a flying waddle as they came squabbling through the mud and straw to shovel up their food.

Best of all he loved the horses and soon came to know each one by name, Charger, Long-legs, Eagle, Gipsy, Speedwell. He would save small scraps from his dinner and feel their soft lips as they nuzzled it off his flat hand. He liked to brush them down and watch them eagerly nosing in the manger after a hard day's work plodding up and down the furrows.

Gipsy was the one he had to watch. If his back was turned she would give him a sharp nip. John thought she only did it for fun, but Tom 'Hatchet', smoking his clay pipe upside down, said she was 'a nasty bit o'stuff' as he spit and poured down his ale.

He was helping one day in the sheep pens, when 'Hatchet' came out with a tiny lamb and threw it down on the straw. It seemed to be all legs and wobbled feebly as it struggled to its feet.

'It'll die,' he said casually, 'unless somebody finds time to hand-feed it. No mother.' He went on. 'There's one in there with a dead young 'un. I put its skin on this, but she still won't suckle it,' and he pushed back his cap and scratched his head.

'Tell you what,' he said, 'take it home and give it a try. Yer can have milk each day with some over for yerselves as well.'

John picked up the little woolly body. 'Don't worry if it dies. It's a weakly runt anyway.'

So John went home that evening with the lamb in his arms and an old tankard of milk for its food.

'Oh poor little thing,' said Beth as she put it by the fire and cuddled it.

It was too young to drink from a porringer so John got an old cloth stocking, soaked it in the milk and pushed it into

'Tell you what,' said Old 'Hatchet', 'take it home and give it a try. Don't worry if it dies. It's a weakly runt anyway.'

its mouth.

'It's sucking it!' cried Charley gleefully and before long it was sleeping near the warm hearth, its little fleeced sides rising and falling as it breathed.

They immediately christened it 'Woolly' and in a couple of weeks or so, it was drinking milk from a basin, following them in and out of the house like a dog and doing joyful leaps and frolics around the garden.

The farm was not the only busy place at this time. There was great activity also at the Manor, for preparations had to be completed for the great Ball on the second of May when all the gentry from miles around would be arriving in their coaches for a magnificent banquet and there would be feasting and dancing far into the night.

Beth was kept hard at work, not only washing-up and preparing vegetables, but helping Lydia, Anna and Deborah, the housemaids. There were windows to be cleaned, floors, furniture and wooden panelling polished, and silver, brass and pewter rubbed till it sparkled and shone, for Sir Aldwig was very proud of his possessions. On the last evening of April, John, Beth and Charley were at home doing their end-of-day jobs – John chopping wood for tomorrow's fire, Beth clearing up from supper, Charley feeding Woolly and the rabbits.

There was a knock on the door and Beth ran to open it. 'Martha!' she cried, surprised and delighted. 'How good it is to see you back again!'

Martha came in smiling and sat for a while telling them about her brother and his wife who was now much improved and, best of all how she had visited their father several times in prison. She told how he had been very ill with gaol fever and although still weak was much better adding that the gaoler had been more than kind to him. 'He enquired about you all constantly,' she said. 'I think during his illness he has thought and worried about you more than ever before. And oh,' she added, diving into her large bag, 'he has sent some more laces for you to sell.'

Sammy was especially pleased to be back and was hopping about from one foot to the other and trying with his own weird noises to tell them what he had been doing. They in their turn had lots to tell Martha, especially Beth, about her work at the Manor.

'All the servants are very friendly except Goodwife Vialls, and cook is sometimes sharp and cross.'

'Oh Mistress Vials is all right,' Martha assured her. 'Do not mind her. It's her job to see everyone else does theirs. She gets blamed if they don't. And as for cook – well, she has a lot on her plate.'

'Is that why she's so fat?' asked Charley. They all looked at him.

'Because she has a lot on her plate,' he persisted.

Everyone laughed, Sammy more than anyone, jumping from one foot to the other and waving his feather-decked hat in the air. Martha rose.

' 'Tis time we were home,' she said. 'I shall be going to the Manor tomorrow. They will need all the extra help they can get to prepare for the May Ball.'

' 'Twill be good to have thee there.' Beth was overjoyed.

They had talked till late and John insisted, tired though he was, that he carried Martha's luggage and went home with her, for it was a fair step up to Underwood Common and lonely on a dark night. For this Martha was grateful. 'I am so glad to be back with you all,' she smiled.

Bright sun greeted the First of May. Beth was at the Manor by seven o'clock but Martha was there before her, neat and trim as always with her white coif and collar and her overskirt tucked up for work, showing her red stammel petticoat underneath.

'The table in the dining room has to be set for tomorrow,' Martha told her. 'I am to help Goodwife Vialls along with Lydia and Deborah, and I have persuaded her that you would be useful fetching and carrying.'

Beth was pleased for it meant she would be working with Martha. She had never been beyond the kitchen before and that had amazed her, but she had a bigger surprise when she entered the great dining chamber. It sparkled with colour as the sun shone through the stained glass windows. All round the room were paintings of the family, sconces on the walls held real wax candles and at one side was what Martha called a 'new-fangled sideboard'. It was of carved oak and displaying some of the silver Beth had helped to polish. She thought it looked like two tables, one on top of the other.

Martha was at the Manor before seven, neat and trim as always in her white coif and collar and her overskirt tucked up for work.

What really took her eye however, were the rugs on the floor, beautiful rugs, like some Martha said her husband used to bring back from the East on his ship. Beth walked round them. 'They're too good to walk on,' she said, and thought of the rushes on their floor at home.

On one side was a huge stone fireplace and down the centre of the long room, an oak dining table. Lydia and Deborah had just spread over it a snowy linen cloth with deep fringing and Beth, resting the cutlery tray on the edge, watched fascinated as they folded napkins into the shape of ships under the critical eye of Goodwife Vialls.

'Wake up Beth Ponder, set down the cutlery and fetch other things from the kitchen!'

All round the table were carved oak chairs with velvet cushions on them and Martha was putting pewter plates, a napkin and a knife fork and spoon, by each place. That was something that made Beth stare, not only was the cutlery of glistening silver, but she had never seen a fork before. They had two prongs and reminded her of a hay-fork. Something else puzzled her, the knives were rounded at the end. Theirs at home were pointed so they could stab the pieces of meat with them.

'Perhaps *they* pick up the meat with the fork,' she thought. Martha was putting silver and glass wine flagons on the table now and glass goblets by each place.

'Beth!' Lydia was calling her. 'Come with me. I'm going to bring in the big salt.'

'The one that looks like a galleon?' asked Beth.

Lydia nodded. 'You take in the smaller hourglass ones and the pepper boxes. Be careful how you carry them.'

They had done as much as they could in the dining room for that day and Lydia and Deborah moved off to get the bedrooms ready for some of the guests would be staying the night. Martha and Beth went back to their usual tasks, Beth to her washing up and Martha helping Cook.

There was a mouthwatering aroma of roasting meat, of pies and pasties, wafting round the kitchen. Beth stared in amazement at the quantities of cream from the bowls in the dairy and eggs from the chickens and dovecotes, that were going into the sauces being mixed with thyme, lavender, mint and rosemary.

'Beth Ponder!' The cook spoke sharply. 'For goodness sake get on with your work. What a wench you are for staring!'

Martha was making 'coffins', pastry containers which would hold sweets and savouries, and placing them in rows ready for filling. Beth stretched her back as she stopped for a moment her endless job of washing-up. The one-fingered clock in the great entrance hall struck eleven.

'Come here Beth Ponder.' Goodwife Vialls had bustled into the kitchen. 'Let me see if you are neat and tidy.' She eyed her critically. 'You'll do I suppose. Take your pinner off. Lady Margaret always has her chocolate at eleven and she specially asked that you should take it to her this morning – goodness knows why. Martha, show her the way.'

Martha dusted flour off her hands while Beth put on a white apron and they went through the great hall, smelling of beeswax and bowls of herbs and flowers, and up the dog-leg staircase, Beth carefully holding the pipkin of hot chocolate. She was a little fearful.

'Why does she want to see me?'

'You will soon know,' was Martha's reply. 'That is her room.' She pointed to a heavy oak door.

Beth gave a timid knock and a voice, which sounded far away, bade her enter. 'Ah, my chocolate – yes – put it there,' and she pointed to her writing table at the foot of a carved four-poster bed, 'Come here and let me look at you. So you are Elizabeth Ponder and your father is in Northampton Gaol for preaching and holding prayer meetings.'

'Yes, my lady.'

'You have two brothers but no mother I believe.'

Beth nodded.

'How are you managing to live?'

'My father left us a little money, my two brothers are working at Farmer Thacker's and I have come here your ladyship.'

'Sir Aldwig told me you were a comely child and we wondered if you would like to live at the Manor to help Tilly and learn from her how to be a lady's maid. You would be taught to sew and embroider so that you could make and alter gowns for myself and my daughters, learn how to dress our hair and assist with our make-up. My youngest daughter is only a little taller than you are and there must be some of her older dresses that would fit you.'

Beth was dumfounded. Live at the Manor! Wear beautiful dresses! Never be hungry. She thought she must be dreaming. But no, there was Lady Margaret looking at her. There was the four-poster bed with its red velvet hangings and embroidered silk bed cover and there was the hot chocolate steaming in the pipkin.

'Of course you need time to think about it. Talk it over with your older brother and tell me tomorrow – no, not tomorrow – that is the May Ball of course. It will do in a few days time – and remember you would not be far from home and could go there often.' A shaft of sunlight came through the window making Beth's hair shine like gold as it fell from under her white coif.

'You're a pretty girl Elizabeth,' said Lady Margaret looking at her hair and wild rose complexion. 'Why don't you starch your apron and collar? You would look much smarter.'

'Oh no, my lady – if you please my lady, my father says I must not. He says starch is the Devil's liquor.'

Lady Margaret laughed. 'Elizabeth my dear,' she said quite kindly, 'you are growing up, you must not be dominated by your father's ideas for ever.'

'He is a very good man your ladyship.'

'That may be so, but the time will come when you must think for yourself. Go now, and come and see me in a few days.'

Beth curtsied as she went out and closed the door, her mind was in a whirl as she told Martha about the interview. 'It would be a splendid chance for you, but you'll have to think about it carefully,' was her reply.

For the rest of the morning Beth went about her work in a dream. How wonderful it would be to live at the Manor, to wear pretty clothes – Beth loved pretty clothes. And then she thought of John and young Charley. What would they do without her? But had not Lady Margaret said she could go home often?

She was free that afternoon for she would have to work extra late on the evening of the Ball. She went out from the Manor House walking on air, along Church Lane and into the Market place. There had been great activity in the whole village during the last week. Winter had gone and all good housewives

Beth often went to the baker's on the Market Hill.
Today she was walking on air.

had been cleaning out its last remains from their cottages, getting rid of dirty rushes from floors and strewing their chambers with sweet-smelling herbs.

May Day was always a great public holiday and everybody who could walk, had been up with the dawn, excitedly off to the woods and commons 'a-maying'. They had brought back branches of Goat Willow catkins, 'Pussy Willow' the children called it, along with armfuls of flowers to decorate the church, the May Queen's cart and their cottages. The may was not fully in flower on the hawthorns but the black-thorns flung out their starrywhite blossoms in abundance and laughed at the sun.

Even before Beth reached Market Hill, she could hear the noise. Rowell's May Day holiday was in full swing. Wandering actors had erected a wooden stage and were performing what looked like a play about Robin Hood and Maid Marian to the cheers claps and boos of the crowd standing there. But the players were not the only attraction. Clowns, jugglers, wrestlers, tumblers, high-wire walkers, and dancers, all were competing for attention. Across Tresham Street, the Woolpack Tavern was doing a roaring trade. All were determined on merry-making, frolic and foolery.

The May Queen, a girl Beth knew by sight, sat high up on a decorated farm cart, gaily dressed and crowned with flowers as she 'presided over' the sports and festivities.

Beth watched for a while and then made her way to the village green where there were Morris dancers and a maypole painted with spiral stripes of different colours and decorated with flowers and gay streamers. She was fascinated by the way the dancers wove and unwove the ribbons around the pole, envious of their pretty dresses and carefree laughter.

As she stood there she was aware of someone close by her. She turned to look and saw a powerfully built man in a tall black sugar-loaf hat and a long black sleeveless coat (like dons wear today) over his doublet and hose. His little pointed beard and moustaches moved in a funny sort of way and his eyes twinkled as he looked down at her.

'You are not joining in with the fun?'

'No sir,' Beth shook her head.

'I thought everyone did on May Day.'

'My family are Puritans sir. My father says sports and wrestling, merrymaking and dancing are inventions of the Devil, that play-actors are wanton sons of idleness and that our belief in God should tell us these things are evil.'

He looked at her in amazement. 'God bless my soul, does he really say all that? But I suppose all Puritans do.'

'Aye sir, I think so.'

'What is your name?'

'Beth Ponder, an' it please thee sir.'

'Well Beth, I should join in the fun if I were you on this beautiful May day, another year your Puritan Cromwell will have forbidden all this merrymaking. I believe in God too but I have a dictum I often repeat to myself – I say, 'This is the day that the Lord has made, I will rejoice and be glad in it.' I find it useful to remember.' He smiled down at her, then turning on his heels, strode off, his black sleeveless coat flapping in the breeze.

'God give thee good day sir,' said Beth, but she was speaking to thin air, he had already gone.

She did not move but she was not watching the dancers any more for her mind had gone back to the old witch. 'You will have sorrow, but you will have joy, and before long a tall dark man will come into your life who will be a very good friend to you. He will be wearing a long black cloak and a black sugarloaf hat.' Was this the tall dark stranger? And if so who was he? Would she ever see him again? But it was too late to find out, he had gone, and anyway her mind was still on Lady Margaret.

May Day or not, the farm had to go on and John came home, tired as usual, from a hard day's work. He was surprised to see Beth gay and fresh, singing as she got the evening meal.

'Hast thou not had a busy day?' he asked as he sat down and pulled off his buskins.

Beth could contain herself no longer and out came the whole story of her talk with Lady Margaret. John listened in silence. He had feared something like this from the first day when Beth had been so excited about the Manor House kitchen.

'Of course thou must decide for thyself – but what dost thou think father would say?' he asked quietly.

'I am growing up John and should now begin to think for

myself.' He detected a note in her voice he had never heard before.

That night Beth lay awake in the darkness. She knew in her *heart* what her father would say, and some words of his came back to her – 'If ever thou art tempted by the Devil, as thou surely will be sometime, look Him straight in the eye and say, 'Get thou behind me Satan.'

'But how am I to know this is the Devil? Perhaps it is God showing me the way to a better life,' she argued to herself.

The night outside had been dark but just then the moon came full and brilliant, like a great yellow cheese, from behind the swift clouds. The Old Man sent down a smile of brightness on her as she lay in bed.

Beth closed her eyes. 'I think about it all tomorrow,' she decided as she fell asleep.

'He will be wearing a long black cloak and a black sugar-loaf hat.'
Was this the tall dark stranger? And if so who was he?

CHAPTER

8

The great May Ball
Beth meets John Bunyan.
Charley in trouble again.
Beth loses her job.

'Why!' Beth exclaimed, 'Thou art John Bunyan from Bedford.'

The day of the great ball arrived.

It was still dark when Beth woke but John had already gone. Charley was still asleep. His 'scaring' job had finished but by arrangement with the ostler at the Manor House stables he was to come and hold the guest's coach horses as they arrived. Dawn broke as Beth left their cottage. Faint clouds like mare's tails drifted across the apple-pink of daybreak and the morning freshness was shimmering with bird song. As she walked up the long drive to the Manor House – a way she sometimes took – she was hit by shafts of sunlight through the limes and chestnuts and the South wind was full of the scent of thyme and clover.

She took a deep breath. She must not think about Lady Margaret's offer just now she decided, for today, the day of the great May Ball, she expected every minute to be filled with fetching and carrying, with back-breaking hours at the long stone sink, scouring greasy dishes and trenchers, pans and platters and lugging hot water from the scullery copper. To her delight however, two other village girls had been hired for the day to do the washing-up which left Beth free to help Martha and cook in the kitchen.

During the morning family coaches began to arrive, beautiful coaches whose framework was covered in painted leather and varnished, driven by their liveried coachmen.

Sir Aldwig and Lady DuVayne were at the front entrance, with its coat of arms above, to meet them with friendly words of welcome. The ladies stepped down in their velvets and laces, caperons on their heads and wearing fur collars and muffs against the cool morning air.

'I trust you had a good journey and did not encounter robbers and highwaymen.' It was Lady Margaret acknowledging the gentlemen, each one cutting a dash with their long beribboned hair, their many buttons and braidings and their heeled and buckled shoes, as they doffed their cocked hats, resplendent with feathers and ribbon loops.

'You did not get stuck in the sloughs I hope or the horses stumble in the plaguey rabbit holes,' came the deep voice of Sir Aldwig.

'Indeed,' Lady Margaret rejoined, 'travelling is so difficult and dangerous nowadays. We do hope you can stay for the ball this evening.'

During the morning family coaches began to arrive, beautiful coaches whose framework was covered in painted leather and varnished, driven by their liveried coachmen

Beth managed to get a quick glance now and again as she came and went with things for the table or hot chocolate for the early arrivals.

The Squire's daughters were tripping about, their colourful silk and taffeta gowns rustling as they went, pushing up their puffed sleeves and making sure the low necklines were showing off their white shoulders and the pearls on their long slender necks. The sight of them worried Beth. If she became their maid, would she ever be able to make dresses like that, or even alter them. How clever Tilly must be. And their hair! Abigale and Alianore had a wired style with their curls standing away on each side of their faces, while Joan had hers in ringlets that reached to her shoulders.

Precisely as the clock, on its bracket in the entrance hall, struck one, the loud gong sounded. Family and guests came from all parts of the house and garden and converged on the great dining chamber, walking over those rugs Beth thought were too grand to have feet on, and sitting down at the massive oak table.

And then, oh what a chattering and laughing and clinking of Venetian glasses there was as they drank to the health of Sir Aldwig and Lady Margaret, to their beautiful daughters, to the May Ball, to anything and everything, filling up again and again from the flagons before them; while the servants staggered in with fat cocks stewed in marrow bones, turkey, roast duck with mushrooms and artichokes, shoulders of mutton with oyster sauce, roast pork, cold goose pie, venison pasties.

Every fire, every spit, every cauldron, every oven, every body, had worked to capacity that morning. The servants, many of them hired for the day, made short work of the dishes that came back, some quite untouched.

Following the first part of the meal were the sweetmeats, comfits made from preserved fruits and even flowers, dipped in melted sugar. There was eringo, the candied root of sea-holly, perfumed to sweeten the breath, marchpane, made with almonds, walnuts, sugar and flour, all served in Martha's 'coffins' and of course, some of her gingerbread.

By three o'clock the last draughts of spiced wine were tipped up and the guests staggered out, the females with Lady Margaret and the gentlemen with Sir Aldwig, to smoke, laugh,

The Squire's daughters were tripping about, their colourful silk and taffeta gowns rustling as they went.

The Great May Ball

tell jests, play at cards or dice, discuss the political situation, or just sleep off the effects of too much food and wine.

Then as darkness fell and everyone had recovered somewhat, the company congregated in what they called the Great Chamber with its gallery at one end, where amid a cacophony of noise, the musicians were tuning up their lutes, viols, flageolets and hauboys ready for the dancing.

The room was a blaze of light and colour. Light from the wax candles in the sconces, from the great chandelier that hung from the ceiling and from the giant candelabra standing in each corner, Colour from the costumes and dresses that were soon whirling, twisting, and leaping to the lively dances.

Lady Margaret, serene and beautiful in her pale green taffeta gown with its deep collar of richest point lace and its long puffed sleeves, moved like a stately galleon among her guests. Not one of the tiny curls outlining her face was awry and the flattering light of a hundred candles glinted softly on her deep chestnut hair and the pearls at her neck and ears.

Beth, peeping through a crack in the door, thought she had never seen a sight so wonderful. She would not even try to tell John about it. He would never understand, and if he did, would not approve. It had been arranged that Sammy should stay with John and Charley that night, for the ball would go on till the early hours and Beth and Martha were to sleep at the Manor.

It was almost two of the clock when they climbed wearily up the back stairs to one of the small rooms at the top of the house. Some guests were just departing and as Beth peered down out of the tiny attic window, she could see a coach with four white horses, clip-clopping off into the moonlight and disappearing between the trees of the long drive.

'Martha,' said Beth turning to her. But Martha was in bed and already asleep.

'I wanted to talk to her,' she thought, 'but never mind, it will do in the morning.'

It had been such a day, that, as she slept, she was still pushing through crowds with great trenchers of food. Sometimes she was trying to reach the guests with hot chocolate and could never quite get to them, or Lady Margaret was angrily pointing to the table – it had all to be cleared and washed up before

Lady Margaret, serene and beautiful, moved like a stately galleon among her guests.

she could go. And then the music of the dances whirled about in her head and she was surrounded by a kaleidoscope of colour, in a sea of satin and silk, velvet and taffeta, mixed up with long fringed breeches, buttons, braids, lace, flowing hair, pointed beards and moustaches; and to the rhythm of the volta, the galliard and the stately pavan, she could hear the tapping high heels of elaborately embroidered shoes.

Suddenly she woke up. It was still dark. Yes, she could still hear the tapping to the beat of the music – but no, it was Lydia and Deborah clattering along the wooden boards outside the bedroom shouting it was time to get up – another busy day was beginning. Dressing had to be done quickly but Beth managed a few words with Martha about Lady Margaret's offer.

'Talk it over with John' was her advice.

'But he won't talk or listen,' said Beth despairingly, 'What would'st thou do Martha? I have none other to ask but thee.'

'You know I think a great deal of you Beth. You are one of the kindest people I know and one of the most sensible. When you have really thought this out, I know you will make the right decision. But come, we must go.'

Beth was disappointed. It was not the answer she wanted.

Down in the kitchen it was a day of clearing up. The scullion boys were busy cleaning out the great heaps of ashes from yesterday's fires, there were still greasy pots and pans to scour and the endless washing-up. There was breakfast to be served to the family and to those guests who had stayed overnight, rooms to be cleared and cleaned.

As Beth was going from the kitchen to the dining chamber, Tilly rushed past her in the great hall and up the staircase. She was usually pleasant and had a smile and a nod for her, but today she said nothing and seemed to be crying.

Later that morning Beth went upstairs with Lydia to help her make beds. Passing by Abigale's room, the door was ajar and from inside came loud voices.

'Tilly, come and arrange my hair, and *do* make it look better than yesterday.'

'Tilly, you must alter this, I want the latest fashion. Make this with virago sleeves, a deep lace collar and embroidery on the jacket.'

'NO! You silly Tilly, not like that – you deserve to have your wages stopped. We will tell our mother you are no good – you –' They were out of earshot now and Beth looked at Lydia. She shrugged her shoulders.

'The young mistresses can be very trying sometimes,' she commented.

Not long after this, Beth was sent to the courtyard at the back of the house with some damaged skillets, for the travelling tinker had arrived and would mend them. When she got there, he was already setting up his brazier, a tall, strong-boned man with a ruddy face and sparkling eyes, singing snatches of song as he heated his soldering irons.

'Why!' Beth exclaimed, 'Thou art John Bunyan from Bedford. I remember thee coming once before and talking with my father, Nathaniel Ponder, the shoemaker.'

The tinker looked hard at her. 'Thou hast a good memory little mistress, 'tis two or three years since I came this way, but I do remember talking to a cordwainer. Is he well?'

'Alas sir, I hope so, but he is even now in Northampton Gaol for preaching.' He looked at her with those sparkling eyes.

'I remember – he talked to me about this life being er – what did he call it? – I know, Vanity Fair, that was it. I can't remember all he said, but something about we were all travelling in the end to what he called the Celestial City.'

'That was my father,' Beth nodded sadly.

'I have this year married a young woman much like him,' John Bunyan laughed. 'She reads to me from the Bible every day and would have me to church the whole of Sunday – but oh, ten thousands hells and the Devil take me, I love to ring the bells and play tip-cat and sport with the lads on the village green. Do not mistake me, however, little mistress, your father is a fine man.'

His skilful hands filled up the hole in the skillet. 'That's something,' he mused, 'I would not be able to do – go to prison for a belief.'

'I must be off,' said Beth, 'thou hast almost finished and I have to bring thee some brass and copper to mend.'

Going back to the house she stopped, for there was a hullabaloo near the coach house and stables. Joan, the Squire's youngest daughter, had her dog on a lead, beating it viciously and unmercifully with a whip, until the poor creature, bruised and bleeding, cowered down on the ground, its tail between its legs.

Beth felt her anger rising but dared not interfer or the whip would have fallen on her. She could not forget it however, for a long time afterwards.

She worked each day that week at her usual duties in the kitchen. Once, in the hall, she came face to face with a tall dark man wearing a long black cloak with a sugar-loaf hat in his hand – the very same one who had spoken to her on May Day.

'What are you doing here, Little Puritan?' he smiled.

'I work in the kitchen sir,' she answered. He nodded and disappeared into Sir Aldwig's library.

Lady DuVayne had not sent for her again. 'Perhaps she has forgotten all about it,' thought Beth. Nor had any more been said at home.

One evening when she got back rather late, John was there before her. 'I've sent Charley to bed,' was his greeting.

'Not without his supper John!' Although he gave her a lot of trouble, Beth always defended him.

'Yes, without his supper – look at that!' and he pointed to a heap of clothes, wet and thick with mud. 'Says he fell into Slade Brook – just look at his shoes and hosen.'

Beth climbed the stairs. 'What hast thou been doing Charley? Just because John and I have to be away all day, doesn't mean thou can run wild and get into all sorts of mischief.'

Charley burst into tears. That was very unusual for him and Beth put her arm round his shoulders. 'Where hast thou been?' she repeated.

Although Charley was often naughty and got into mischief, he was never untruthful. 'To the fish ponds in the Manor park,' came the tearful reply.

'But that was trespassing – how did you get there?' She knew it could not be by the main gates. They were locked and unlocked by the keeper.

'Down under the hump-backed bridge. I wanted to catch a fish so we could have it to eat.'

'Charley! It's very hard to make both ends meet and sometimes we've been hungry but that would be stealing – a thing we've never done. Beside, thou must have a proper line to catch fish.'

'I made one with a willow stick and a worm tied on to it. I could see the fish – trout I think they are – I felt a tug and thought I'd got it, so I pulled the stick out so fast it went right over my head.'

'With or without the fish?'

'Without – but I caught something else.'

'Something else?' Beth looked surprised.

Charley gave a little half smile. 'Baillif Foggarty's cocked hat. It came off and rolled into the water.'

'Oh Charley! So you were caught!'

'No, I dashed back to the bridge before he could do anything and that's when I got dirty – I fell down by the water side where it was all slippery mud, but I got away.'

'And if Baillif Foggarty recognised thee, he'll be coming here – he's just looking for an excuse to turn us out.'

'No he won't, for he was shouting, 'Hi, you scoundrel – come here again and you'll feel my stickel round your ears,' but he didn't say my name and he's short-sighted anyway.'

'Oh Charley, thee'll be the death of me,' said Beth despairingly, and she put her head in her hands.

'Beth!' She looked up. 'I can write my name now. I've been practising in the mud down by Slade Brook – and Beth – I'm so hungry.'

She looked at him, still dirty and tear stained. How could she be cross? 'John said, "No supper", but I'll try to bring thee a bite when he's gone outside.'

'Oh dear,' she thought to herself as she went downstairs, 'he's sure to get into trouble if we are away from home all day.'

There was still no word from Lady Margaret until one afternoon, carrying something to the dining chamber for cook, Beth met her in the hall. 'Ah, Elizabeth Ponder,' Lady Margaret was smiling. 'When can Tilly start to make you into a first class lady's maid?'

Beth curtsied and replied quietly, 'If it please your Ladyship, I have decided not to accept your offer.'

Lady Margaret was not used to being denied anything. She looked at Beth with amazed anger in her eyes. She had offered to take this wretched cordwainer's wench into her home, feed her, clothe her and have her taught, and here she was daring to spurn her offer. She walked on haughtily but turned on the first step of the staircase.

'I did not think beggars could be choosers,' she said icily. 'Very well, your job here at the Manor will end today. Get your wages from Goodwife Vialls and be gone. There are plenty of other village girls who will be glad to come.'

Beth was taken aback. She had not expected to lose her kitchen job. Martha was not there that day and there was no one to tell but cook. She was busy as usual and her only comment was, 'Ah 'tis a pity – thee's a willing wench. Here's a bit 'o meat pasty to take with thee.'

Goodwife Vialls gave her the wages that were due and when evening came, she took off her pinner and laid it by, donned her capa and left the Manor House with all its hard work but its many attractions, for ever she felt, and not without regret.

As she walked home the evening sun was still shining, but great storm clouds, black as ash buds, massed in the sky. Suddenly from the heart of the clouds came a javlin thrust of lightning and almost immediately a crack of thunder as though the earth had split apart. It boomed and rolled round the sky again and again before it died away. Beth started to run as a deluge of rain came down and poured off the gutterless roofs.

Charley was staying the night with Martha and Sammy. John was home early from the farm and had escaped the storm. 'I've some news for thee Beth,' he said, carrying in a bundle of faggots to stoke up the fire. She looked up from drying herslef. 'Farmer Thacker has told me that after haymaking, there will be no more jobs for me till harvest time.'

Beth was abashed. 'And I've some news for thee John. I have refused Lady Margaret's offer.'

John's face brightened. 'But she says I can no longer work there!'

She expected him to be dismayed, but he was still smiling. 'Come right by the fire and get properly dry,' he said.

'There's nothing to smile about,' Beth commented. 'With no job for either of us, what shall we do?'

But John was still smiling. 'I'm glad thou art finished at the Manor. Thou would'st have grown farther and farther away from us with all thy fine clothes and travel. We would have managed somehow, but thou would never have been happy

Beth, and that's what I was most worried about. Their way of life is not ours.'

'But John, how shall we live?'

'We have spent less on food lately so what we have saved in the 'Hidey' box will help us on for a while – besides I have another surprise for thee. My job with Farmer Thacker may soon be finished, but I've got another – one that will give me all the pleasure in the world.' Beth looked up in surprise.

'It's at the Crown Inn working with Amos, the ostler there, looking after all the horses – that is something I shall really enjoy. Besides I shall get more pay, four pence a day instead of three, and some food. And,' John added, 'it will soon be Rowell Fair and we shall be able to sell more of father's laces.'

Beth was dry now and feeling more cheerful. 'Well, there's lots of jobs to be done here,' she said. 'Perhaps tomorrow I'll clear out all the old floor rushes and get some nice, new, sweet-smelling ones.'

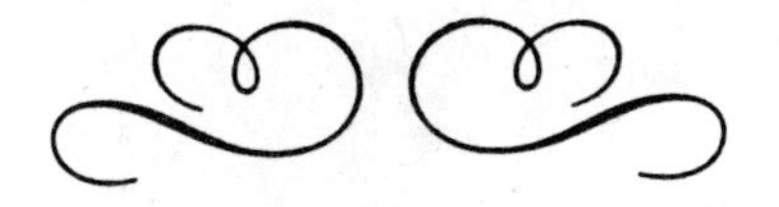

CHAPTER

9

John leaves Farmer Thacker's and goes to the Crown Inn as an ostler.
Martha is a great help to Beth.
Rowell Fair and the tall dark stranger again.

Proclamation of the Fair

The next few weeks of May were busy ones at the farm and John was working from dawn to dusk. It was 'all hands to the wheel' as Old Tom 'Hatchet' said, even to the youngest, following the skilled cutters with their long scythes and cocking the cut grass into heaps as quickly as possible out of the sun's rays which would spoil it. By luck the weather was dull, but it was windy and the hay flew into the horses, onto the wagons, right over the wagons, everywhere. The raking and scraping went on furiously, and they tried to catch forkfuls as the wind whirled it away.

At noon on his last day, John threw himself thankfully down and with the other sun-tanned labourers, ate his food under the shade of the limes. Lying on his back, surrounded by the heavy scent of hay, he was lulled by the hum of nectar-seeking bees. Old 'Hatchet' puffed away at his upturned pipe and delivered some of his weather lore.

'A swarm o'bees in May is worth a load of hay,' he commented. 'But there ain't bin enough rain – Water in May and there'll be bread all through the year.' He spit and poured down his ale. And then it was back to work till sunset. John was tired by this time and the creek of the haywain wheels, as they rolled back to the farm, was a pleasant sound to him.

His work at the farm had been hard. He knew his new job at the Crown Inn would be hard too, but he was sure it would be enjoyable and he was looking forward to it.

Beth, glad of her freedom again, went off to the fields and commons, the woods and the waterside, sometimes with Charley and often with Sammy following behind, to collect new rushes and fragrant herbs. It was wonderful to be out in the fresh May air after being cooped up at the Manor. The dainty white stars of anemones carpeted the woodland floor, and the pale green foliage of the beeches cast a hundred shadows on the carpet of young ferns and the haze of bluebells underneath. Birds flitting from spray to spray of hawthorn, scattered its pink and white petals as they went.

Near Slade Brook they gathered rushes. Yellow marsh marigolds grew there and Beth thought of her father – 'My little Marybud', he used to say. In the damp places also, grew the lilac flowers of ladys-smock, the tall yellow flags, with their leaves like sword blades, forget-me-nots and meadowsweet. In the open pastures they picked cowslips to make a drink, keck beloved by the rabbits, and comfrey leaves for fomentations. Charley picked yellow buttercups and held them under all their chins to see if they 'liked butter'. Sometimes Beth made a tiny posy of heartsease (the wild pansy with a little face) of scarlet pimpernel (the poor man's weather glass, because it closes when rain is about) and of bright blue bird's eye – fairy flowers she called them. Sometimes they sat by the water watching the mayflies dance over it, and the fish rise to take them as they touched the surface, or Charley looked for newt or frog spawn that blackened the shallows of the brook.

Martha often called on her way home from the Manor with left-overs of food cook had given her and she always had some helpful advice.

Beth thought Martha was wonderful with wool. She would get Sammy to collect stray handfuls from the bushes but she also bought it from Farmer Thacker. She would wash it, card it, and spin it on her wheel and then collect plants to dye the yarn. Many a time Beth had seen it hanging up to dry, before she took it to Joe-the-Weaver whose loom seemed to fill his tiny cottage.

One day she brought some yarn for Beth, along with a pair of sticken pins and showed her how to knit. She struggled for a long time for she found it difficult and she was a little more sympathetic with Charley when he was struggling with his reading and writing. She plodded on however, determined to knit a muffler each for John, Charley and Sammy for Christmas.

'But what can I make for father as a present when he comes home?' she wondered.

'Stitch him a cushion to make the settle more comfortable,' Martha suggested. 'I will ask Tilly for any odd bits of material she has from her gown making and I will show you how to stitch them together to make patchwork.' This took a long time and Beth painstakingly worked at it every evening till the light faded. She was better with her needle than her sticken pins.

At last it was finished and when she had stitched it up in the form of a long bag, Martha sent Sammy with a whole lot of her chicken feathers, and what fun they all had trying to get them in. Martha had warned they should do it outside because of

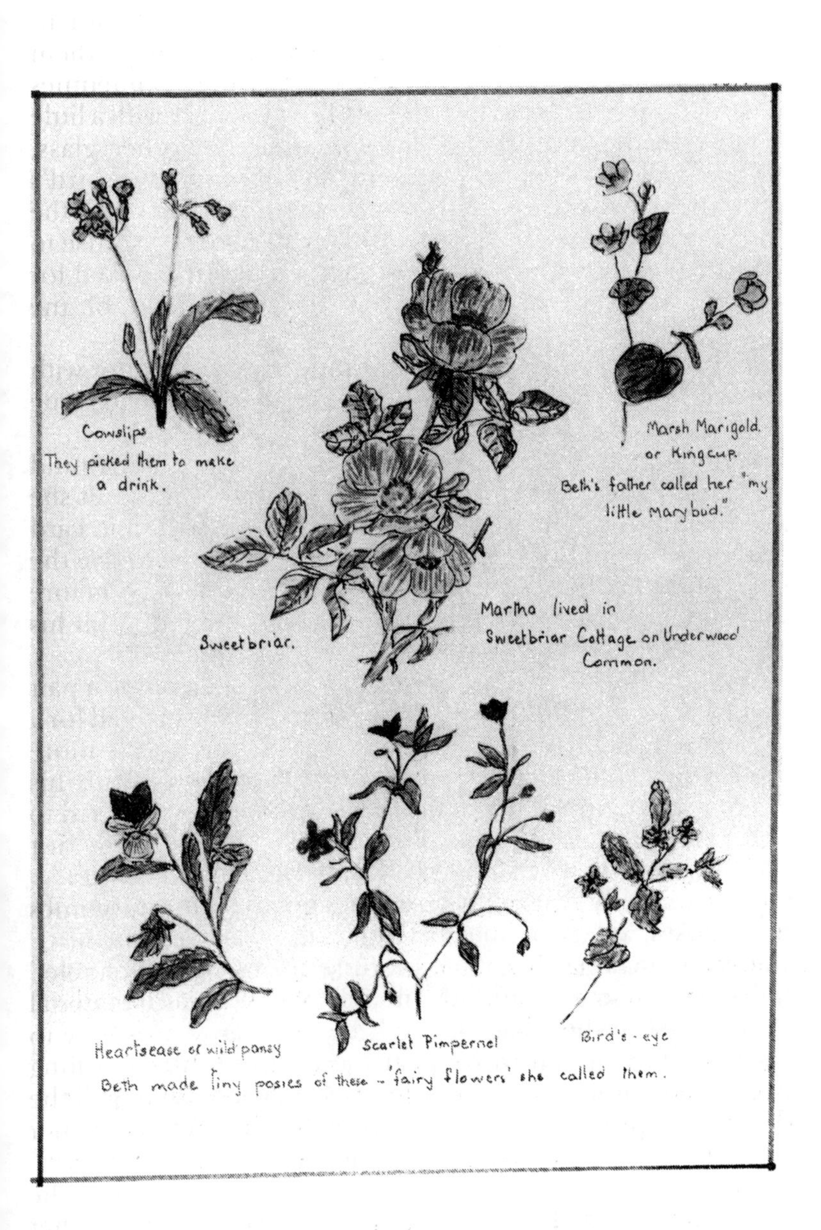
Cowslips
They picked them to make a drink.
Marsh Marigold. or Kingcup.
Beth's father called her "my little Marybud."
Sweetbriar.
Martha lived in Sweetbriar Cottage on Underwood Common.
Heartsease or wild pansy
Scarlet Pimpernel
Bird's-eye
Beth made tiny posies of these - 'fairy flowers' she called them.

Beth struggled for a long time to get the patch-work done for the cushion.

the mess but it was a slightly windy day and the feathers seemed alive, flying everywhere. They got in their eyes and up their noses, till everyone was sneezing, waving their arms wildly and making all sorts of snorting noises. But at last it was finished to Beth's satisfaction and the wayward feathers imprisoned in their bag.

They all thought it was a great success but John wondered what their father would say to its bright colours, so they decided to put it on the settle immediately, 'because it will have got a little dirty by the time he comes home,' said Beth.

So May passed pleasantly enough. There was money for the rent in the 'Hidey' box and a little to spare. With that and John's wages they could manage.

June came with some scorching days and there was a constant hum of bees as they hunted in the nectared clover of West Meadow.

'Hi-yee-ow!' cried Charley one morning as he bumped up and down on one of the wooden stools, pretending to gallop a horse. 'Only one week to the Great Fair!'

'Yes, I know,' came Beth's voice, 'but don't break the stool will you chuck.'

Long before dawn on Fair Monday morning Charley was up – they all were, no one could sleep. There was a full moon, it was as light as day, and the street outside was in an uproar.

It was exciting. Charley rushed outside. Dozens of horses were cantering up the road in a sea of dust, whinnying and snorting, their manes and tails flying. Flocks of terrified, woolly sheep were crazily rushing every way but the right one, baaing in a dozen keys with almost human cries, sending the drovers wild as they jumped, yelled and thumped with their heavy sticks, and herds of cattle went stampeding by, their steaming bodies bumping and their forelegs mounting each other's backs as they were prodded and thawacked and driven along the narrow road; for it was a horse, cattle and sheep Fair as well as a huge market, and a great time to eat, drink and be merry. It only came once a year and all were determined to make the most of it.

By six o'clock, when everybody had been up for hours, it was time to 'Proclaim the Fair.'

The cattle and sheep had gone to Squire's Hill and Sheep Street for the 'Great Sale', and the horses to Castle Hill, where the excited dealers galloped them up and down for the buyers, waving red flags or banging an old iron skillet with their whip-stock behind some young 'galloway', shouting, 'Hi! Hi! Hi! Hooroo! HI! HI! HI! Hooroo! There's a beauty from Timbuctoo!'

The rest of the crowd lined Tresham Street and the Market Place and there was a sea of faces as, dead on six o'clock, riding on a noble steed, came The Lord of the Manor, mace in hand, with a blue ribbon hanging from the 'Proclamation'. Six halberdiers went before him followed by the Yeomanry band on horseback, banging their drums loud enough to awaken the dead in the churchyard.

Hats flew into the air and a great shout went up as Sir

Aldwig began the 'Proclamation' in a thunderous monotone outside the Woolpack Tavern.

'Whereas, heretofore, his late Majesty, King John, did grant to the lords of the Manor of Rowell, the rights to hold a Fair which shall begin on the Monday after the Feast of Holy Trinity, continuing for the space of five days, when it shall be lawful to come, to go, to buy, to sell, all manner of cattle and merchandise by the laws of – '

Beth did not wait to hear any more. She had lost John and Charley somewhere in the crowd and she knew that by the time the 'Proclamation' had been read outside all of the town's taverns, the men would be dead drunk and rolling off their horses and Sir Aldwig would be reading the 'Proclamation' upside down and getting the words all mixed up, with everybody shouting and laughing at them.

She also knew there would be a shout of 'BATTLE!' which was always the signal for a pitched fight between rival bands of apprentices from Kettering and Harborough, with everyone else joining in, and it was not wise to be in the middle of that, when fists and sticks and bags of soot and flour and rotten eggs and mud were flying in all directions.

So she slipped away through the Churchyard back home to have a bite to eat and to get the leather laces she hoped to sell. She tied them carefully onto a stick so they would pull out easily without getting tangled, and left John's on a nail by the door – but none for Charley – she knew him, scatter-brain that he was, he would lose them, with the same old tale afterwards, 'I didn't mean to –'

By the time she got back, a clean white collar and pinner on her brown dress, the Constable and some of the Watch he had hired for the Fair, were sitting by the Market House wall, ruefully rubbing their heads and various other parts that had suffered from the sticks of the 'prentices, but *they* were halfway to Harborough by now, with the Kettering rowdies in hot pursuit.

The Fair proper was just beginning.

Market carts and wagons came rolling in carrying crowds of countryfolk. Farmer's wives, their tall hats on top of their white coifs, riding pillion on horseback behind their husbands. Tradesmen's booths lined the streets, and how the tables groaned with sweetmeats and cheeses, beef and ham, tripe and home-brewed ale, cakes from Banbury, linsey - woolsey, silks and velvets, laces and ribbons and yards of galloon for trimmings, and many were the thieving eyes thereon. There were ladders and ropes, string and timber, piles of hurdles and piles of besoms, willow bowls and spoons from Leicestershire, rakes and shafts from Corby.

'Come buy! Come buy! Come buy!'

'What d'ye lack?'

The noise was deafening. Every boy had a trumpet and every show a drum. There were boxers, conjurors, mountebanks, quack doctors, tumblers, cockfighting, ale drinking and gambling everywhere. You could have your fortune told or pay the piper in the dancing booth. Beth's eyes looked hungrily at the rhubarb tarts being served up with a dash of honey, and the great piles of gingerbread.

'Laces! Laces for your shoon!' she cried. 'Look, Mistress, only two farthings a pair!'

Her small voice was lost in the hubbub, but she did have *some* luck with the farmers and their wives and the country folks who were 'buying in' for next year.

Once she caught sight of John but she could get nowhere near him. Goodness only knew where young Charley was.

By eleven o'clock she had made quite a few sales, so she crouched by the Churchyard wall and counted the money in her little bag. Twelve pennies, but she still had more to sell, so she got up and began her cry again. 'Laces! Laces! Come good masters, strong la. . . .'

Suddenly she was on the ground, her little money bag was snatched from her hand and a ragged, gipsy-looking boy was making off with it. She hardly had time to shout - no one would have heard her anyway - when she saw the boy go sprawling on the cobbles.

He had been tripped by a tall man in a sugar-loaf hat and a long black sleeveless coat over his doublet and hose. Powerfully built, he picked up the boy by the scruff of his neck and took him to Beth.

'Now give it back to her!'

The gipsy threw down the bag and dashed off, glad to be away with no more than a kick on his behind.

'Why, it's my young Puritan again,' he said. 'I should go home if I were you, there's plenty more about like him.' He looked down at her with kindly eyes and his little pointed beard and moustaches moved in a funny sort of way.

Just at that moment John, with a torn smock and a black eye above the freckles, came pushing through the crowd, his coppery hair sticking straight up, laces dangling in one hand. 'Anything wrong Beth?'

'Thou'st been in a fight!'

'Got mixed up with the 'prentices,' John admitted.

This is my brother,' Beth explained.

'Everything's all right now young fellow, but you should take better care of your sister – she nearly lost all her money.'

'A gipsy boy snatched it from me and this gentleman got it back.'

'We do indeed thank thee kindly sir.' said John.

'What did you say your name was?'

'Ponder sir, we live in Rowell.'

'Ponder – Ponder – ah, that's right, and it is your father who is in Northampton Gaol for his religious ideas?' They nodded, surprised that he knew.

'You are selling laces I see.'

'Yes, father makes them. He is a shoemaker by trade.'

'Many left?' They hastily counted their two lots.

'Four and twenty pairs sir. They're two farthings a pair if it please you master.'

'I'll take them all.'

John's big ears seemed to stick out more than usual and his eyes opened wide – even the black one. They could hardly believe their luck as the gentleman counted out twelve pennies.

'I am new in Rowell but I have heard of your father. He should be at home looking after you.'

'He is a fine man – and we are managing.' John pulled himself up to his full height and Beth went and stood beside him.

'*My* name is Owen Ragford. I have recently come to be Master at the Grammar School here, he continued. 'Come and see me if you think I can help any time.' His eyes twinkled and his pointed beard and moustaches moved in that funny sort of way.

As Beth dropped a curtsy and John pulled his forelock, he

nodded, turned on his heel and strode away with the laces, his long black gown flapping as he went.

'Well that was a stroke of luck,' John grinned.

'Yes indeed, he has been a very good friend to us this day.'

'Said his name was Owen Ragford and that he was the new schoolmaster.'

'I've seen him before,' Beth added, 'he came into the Manor House to see Sir Aldwig.'

'Now let's find our Charley before he gets into mischief.' And they plunged off into the crowds.

But Beth was puzzled. Owen Ragford was new in the village. How did Joanna Stephens know he would be there to help just when she needed it? – because she was a witch? – or because she was, as Watercress Willy had said, 'a very wise old woman'?

CHAPTER 10

Owen Ragford offers Beth a job.
Charley goes to his Grammar School.
John gets an extra duty at the Crown.
Travelling Players come to the village.

Everybody was very excited when travelling players came to the village.

July came with its fragrant scents of Summer. Swallows twittered under the eaves of the cottage darting low among the midges overhead. Down Sweetbriar Lane and along Daisybank Footpath, an ancient pack-horse track, masses of pink blackberry flowers gave promise of luscious Autumn berries, and bindweed draped great white bells over the bushes.

Beth, picking her way on the cobbles of Market Hill one afternoon on her way from the bakery, was suddenly aware of someone in front of her. Looking up, there was Owen Ragford smiling down at her in that funny way of his and wriggling his moustaches. 'Beth Ponder by my troth,' he said, 'not working at the Manor today?'

'No sir – I do not work there any more.'

'No? Not dismissed in disgrace, I hope?'

'Oh no sir,' she paused, 'but perhaps you might call it that sir,' and she told him the story of Lady Margaret's offer and her annoyance – anger even – when she had refused it. Owen's eyes opened wide as he tugged at his beard and his moustaches wriggled.

'Oh dear, Lady Margaret would not like that. She's not used to being crossed or denied anything. So you have no work now?'

'No sir, and John has had to leave Farmer Thacker's till come harvest time, but he's helping Amos, the ostler at The Crown. He's always loved horses and they seem to like him,' she added.

'Ah, I know Amos well – I often hire a horse there when I need to ride abroad. Sir Aldwig tells me you have a young brother, what of him?'

'He is a big worry to me sir. When I was at the Manor I was never sure he wasn't into mischief. I give him jobs to do and try to teach him to read and write. I think he could do well if he would only try but he loves to be out of doors "collecting things" as he calls it.'

'What sort of things?'

'Oh you know sir, worms, spiders, beetles, bird's eggs – anything – and then he hides them, upstairs sometimes – he even brought some baby mice in one day!' Owen laughed.

'Sounds as though he would make a good Naturalist.'

There was Owen Ragford smiling down at her in that funny way of his and wriggling his moustaches. 'Beth Ponder by my troth,' he said. 'Not working at the Manor today?'

'I don't know what that is sir, but it would indeed pleasure me if he could read and write.'

Owen was tugging at his beard. 'How would you like a small job at my house?' Beth looked quickly up at him.

'I would pay you the wages you got at the Manor and take young what's-his-name, into my school free of charge.'

Beth's eyes lit up. 'Oh sir, that is indeed kind of you – but will I be able to do the job?' she added quickly.

'Can you read Beth – if I may call you Beth?'

'Oh yes sir, our father taught both John and I.'

'Easily and well?'

'I think so sir – we read the Bible each evening.'

'I have recently married a French lady. We have a house servant but if you could go for an hour or two each day and read to my wife while she works her embroidery, she would be delighted. You would keep her company and it would help to improve her English.' Beth loved reading. This would be wonderful.

'If you are not too busy at this moment I will take you to meet her now.'

The Grammar School, founded in the time of Edward VI and the School House next door to it, stood at the corner of School Lane and Desborough Road. They were built of ironstone salvaged from the remains of an old ruined nunnery which had stood close by. Owen took her up to the front door and inside by a spiral staircase to an upper room.

As they climbed Beth could hear sweet tinkling music, almost like she imagined the fairies made when they danced at midnight, and as Owen opened the door she could see a large room with a handsome oriel window that looked down on the road below and Mistress Ragsdale seated at a small keyboard instrument.

'Playing your virginal today my dear?'

She jumped up as they entered, her bright dark eyes shining. 'Oh my Owen, she cried in her French accent, 'I am so 'appy when I see you, and,' she puckered her pretty face, 'so lonely when you are not here.'

'But my love you know I must be doing my work. Sir Aldwig DuVayne would say, 'No more money, and take it ill indeed if I neglected my schoolmastering. But see here, I have found a young companion for you who will come and talk and read to you.'

As she came toward them, her hands outstretched, Beth thought she had never seen anyone so pretty, so dainty or so tiny, for she barely came up to Owen's broad shoulders. 'That will be très bien! What is your name ma chérie?'

'Beth Ponder if it please thee Mistress.'

'You are a pretty girl Beth - très jolie - and can you read well?'

Marie jumped up as they entered. Beth thought she had never seen anyone so pretty or so dainty.

'I think so, Mistress.'

Owen smiled. 'I will leave you two together,' he said and disappeared.

'And you will come each day?'

'Ay, an' it please thee Mistress.'

'If we are to be friends, you must not call me Mistress'' – my name is Marie.'

She shook her dark curls and walked daintily in her tiny embroidery silk mules, to a high-backed chair. Seating herself, she waved her fan gently to and fro as she asked Beth to sit and have a dish of tea with her.

'I have never had any before,' said Beth doubtfully.

'Then now is the time to try it,' she laughed, a pleasant tinkling little laugh that sounded almost like her virginal.

She poured it from a silver pot into what Beth thought was a small bowl with a shallow dish under it, such pretty, fragile things, like Mistress Ragford herself. It was a new taste to her and she was not sure she liked it, but it would never have done to say so. She watched Marie as she daintily sipped, head slightly on one side, and put it back on its saucer again, and she tried to do the same.

Beth found herself chatting quite easily. She told Marie about her father, about John and Charley. She talked of her job at the Manor and why it ended, and about Martha and Sammy. Marie in her turn said she liked England but was often homesick for Paris. 'That is the chief city of France you know,' she said, 'like London is of England, and it is, oh so beautiful a city. I tell Owen to give up his schoolmastering here in England – I have plenty of money of my own,' and she waved her arms, 'and I want us both to go back to La Belle France for ever!'

'Oh no, Mistress Ragford!'

'*Marie*, Beth!'

'Do not do that – Marie. I am sure the Grammar School would not be the same without him.'

'They would find someone else,' and she shrugged her pretty shoulders.

They were getting on well together and Beth felt already that Marie would be a good friend, though not in the same way as Martha of course. It was arranged when she should come and as she looked round the room with its overflowing bookshelves, she thought how lucky she was and only hoped her reading would please.

She walked home with a light heart that afternoon and John (and Martha, when she called on her way home from the Manor) had to hear the whole story, especially about the tea drinking. They were both delighted, but Charley, listening in

Marie was often playing her virginal when Beth went to read to her.

his favourite place under the table, scowled to himself as he heard the part about his going to school, and decided he would get out of that somehow if he could.

'It is very strange,' said John, 'and thou won't believe this, but I also have been asked today if I can read.' They looked at him in surprise.

'You haven't got another job John?'

'No, the same job, helping Amos, but the host at the Inn has a news-sheet sent from London each week and wants me to read it to his customers, for most of them have never learned how.'

In spite of Charley's determination not to go to Owen Ragford's school, Beth was equally determined that he should. So, on a day Owen had indicated, she took him there to make sure all was well.

The schoolhouse consisted of a large upper room where the boys were taught (and where hung an imposing portrait of Sir Aldwig DuVayne) and two smaller rooms, one a library, the other the Master's room. Over the entrance door, carved in the stone were the words, 'Children obey your parents in the Lord, for this is right.' The bottom part of the building was an arched space where the boys could amuse themselves under cover without getting wet in rainy weather.

Charley soon made friends with a boy called Piers, but quickly learned to keep out of the way of a gang of older bullies whose ringleader was Faulk Foggarty, the Bailiff's son. He found life very different however, from the free one he had been living. No longer could he roam the woods and commons at will. No longer could he lie on his stomach by Slade Brook and watch the fish rise to the swarming gnats, or imagine he was sailing on a leaf down the stream. No longer could he lie on his back in a bed of wild flowers watching birds in their flight or float in imagination on a white billowing cloud as it swept across the blue sky. As he struggled with his reading in English and Latin, writing with a quill pen, and casting accounts, he longed for each Holy-Day when he would be free again for a while, and many a time did Doctor Ragford have to chastise him for not attending.

'Uncultivated minds are not full of flowers. Villainous weeds appear in them and they are the haunt of toads,' he quoted to him.

The schoolhouse consisted of a large upper room where the boys were taught. The bottom part of the building was an arched space for rainy weather.

Beth was enjoying her readings with Marie. They were not the sort of books her father read, the Bible, *Fox's Book of Martyrs, A Plain Man's Pathway to Heaven*, tracts and sermons, but exciting stories about Troy and King Arthur, Chaucer's *Canterbury Tales*, yarns of travel, romance and adventure.

One evening there she remembered with great pleasure. The Ragford's had asked her to help with a little supper party they were having, and afterwards the guests sat round the table singing to the accompaniment of Marie's virginal and Owen's bass viol, and passers-by looked up at the open oriel window as the music floated down to the road below.

Meanwhile John was kept busy at the Crown. There were a great many horses in the stables round the big inn yard and always plenty of trade, Stage wagons, private coaches, post-boys and local citizens wishing to hire, all used them. One day he came home with the news that travelling players had arrived and had got a permit from the Constable to erect a wooden stage on their cart, in the inn yard, and Charley excitedly announced he had seen them going round the village in their gaudy rags and cock-feathered hats, playing a pipe and banging a drum to announce their play. A jester, in clothes of red and yellow, stood outside the inn, shouting, capering and jingling his bells as he waved and banged with a great inflated bladder on the end of a stick.

When Beth came from reading to Marie, a goodly crowd had gathered and the play already begun. She immediately spotted Charley getting one of the best views from the wheel of a cart. So she stood and watched and found herself caught up in the story, booing when the villain stole the hero's wife and lands, cheering when they fought, groaning when the hero had to flee as an outlaw, but cheering again as the Sheriff was hanged and the hero restored to his rightful possessions. The show finished off with a chained bear padding a lumbering dance to the beat of a drum and the shouts and claps of the audience. Suddenly Beth heard a voice above her.

'Inventions of the Devil, masters of vice, teachers of wantonness, sons of idleness – have I remembered it correctly?' It was Owen Ragford, smiling quizzically down at her and wriggling that beard and those moustaches in his own funny sort of way. Hearing his voice, Charley ducked under the nearest pair of legs and disappeared. Beth was nonplussed for a

The Crown Inn was a busy place.

moment hearing the words quoted back to her.

'I noticed you were enjoying the play – that is good, enjoy everything you can in this world my dear Beth – it is a beautiful day – rejoice and be glad in it – remember?' Beth smiled and nodded.

'I remember,' she said.

'I am happy indeed that you and Marie are getting on so well together. She is still rather homesick for France and your visits have given her great pleasure.'

'I enjoy them too.' said Beth, 'and I think my reading is improving every day.'

She had not seen Dr Ragford for some time and ventured to ask him about Charley's progress at school. 'He's getting on like a house on fire,' was his answer.

'Truly sir?'

'Once the fire is lit,' he added, 'it blazes away.' His eyes twinkled and he wriggled his beard and moustaches. Beth was puzzled. 'I do have to do a little fanning of the flames with my birch now and again,' he smiled.

Beth understood and smiled too. Owen had taken off his steeple hat, but now he put it on again, pulled his gown round him and went striding off.

Beth watched him go, she was quite sure now that he was the 'tall dark man' the witch had foretold. She was so happy that Charley was in his capable hands, happy for John doing a job he loved, happy for herself and happy for them all that six months of their year alone had gone and that life seemed a little rosier.

CHAPTER

11

Collecting herbs, berries and nuts with Martha.
Charley and Piers also go 'collecting'.
Sammy and the bees.
Charley and Faulk Foggarty.
Cleaning out the well.

July melted into August with its warm sunny days.

Beth had plenty of time when her reading job was done, to wander round the fields and woods and she and Martha and Sammy often took their food and ate it sitting on a fallen tree trunk or lying in the cool grasses among the twittering birds, the hum of bees in the second crop of white clover and the crickets chirping in the wild thyme.

By Slade Brook the leaves were beginning to show a tinge of grey and yellow on their spikes, wild honeysuckle perfume blew in on the wind, Red Admiral butterflies flitted here and there and settled on the purple crowns of thistles.

Martha made many preserves, and they collected crab apples, sloes, (the black damson-like fruit of the blackthorn) wild strawberries, and elderberries for wine.

'I have heard the elder is a magic tree,' said Beth, as she broke off the bunches of black berries, 'and has a great love for mankind, but that, to be on the safe side, it is wiser to ask its pardon when we cut it.'

'Then we'd better remember to do that,' said Martha smiling, 'for we have picked a basketful this day and we would not like to hurt its feelings or seem ungrateful.'

They left the bunches of haws, now turning from green to red, and the red bryony berries that scrambled over the bushes, to the birds, but picked the scarlet hips to make rosehip jelly. There would be hazel nuts, sweet chestnuts and blackberries aplenty next month.

Charley came with them if it was a Church Holy-Day and there was no school, or he and Piers, (a boy after his own heart who also loved 'collecting') would have a day out together in the woods or commons. Sammy liked to go too, but usually they managed to dodge him and go off by themselves.

On one particular day however, Piers was not there and Beth had sent Charley to fetch faggots and cones for the fire. In that case Sammy was a good help with dragging them back. He loped after Charley in his country smock, his hat decorated with its cock feathers and wild flowers, and off they went to Slade Woods. Charley, as usual, left the hard work to Sammy while *he* went off looking for things to 'collect'.

Once he spied a tawny owl at the top of a tree, but it flew away with a great flapping of wings. And once, a good distance away, he caught sight of Faulk Foggarty and some of his cronies. They were laughing and yelling and ready for any mischief. The two boys were near to a thicket that Charley knew well, for he often kept his 'collectings' in a hollow tree there. Into this he pushed Sammy and put a finger on his lips. They did not come any nearer however, and much to Charley's relief their voices soon died away in the distance. So they crawled out and went on with their wood collecting. Poking about in a bank with one of the sticks, Charley spied a hole.

'Ah, a mousehole,' he thought to himself, but no, bees were going in and out. Sammy loved sweet things, so Charley, mischievous as ever, thought here was a chance to have some fun.

'Come here Sammy!' he called, and Sammy obediently trotted over. 'Do you want some honey?' and he made sucking noises and put his fingers on his tongue. Sammy understood and his face was wreathed in smiles as he waved his arms and hopped from one foot to the other.

'Dig in that hole – there's some there.' And getting a sharp piece of wood, he started it off for him. Sammy set about digging eagerly, while Charley stood a safe distance away.

It was not long before a swarm of excited bees were buzzing about their ruined doorway and Sammy came away shaking his head from side to side. Charley began pelting the hole with fir cones, and to his dismay, the angry creatures came buzzing about *his* head. He tried buffeting wildly with his cap, but this only brought the whole swarm round him and soon he was yelling, with stings on his face, neck and hands.

He ran as hard as he could to get away from them, waving his arms round his head, and rolled in some grass and fern. Sammy came up to him. He was all right. *He* had stood quite still and they had not stung him. So it was he who had to lead the way home, for Charley's face and eyelids were so swollen, he could hardly see out of them.

'That will teach you a lesson,' said John as he dabbed some witchhazel on the stings. 'You must have been aggravating them or they would have left you alone – see Sammy is all right.'

'I must be a lot sweeter than he is,' was Charley's wry comment.

A couple of weeks after this, Charley took Piers into the

wood to see if the tawny owl was still in the same tree.

'There it is!' Charley whispered as they crept silently nearer. 'And there it goes!' he cried. 'Something must have disturbed it!'

There was a dull thud and a bundle of feathers dropped to the ground. It was the owl. The body quivered, and then was still.

'It's dead!' Charley's voice expressed amazement, sorrow and disbelief.

There was a scuffling in the dead leaves, twigs snapped, the hazel copse parted and there stood Faulk Foggarty, leering and dangling a sling, followed by several of his gang. Piers dashed off.

'Thee'st a murderer!' Charley exploded and rushed at him with a stick he was holding which left its mark across Foggarty's face.

'You'll pay for this you wry-necked potherd of a Puritan Ponder,' he yelled, wiping his face and taking aim with his sling. Charley glanced round. Should he escape if he could? He was hopelessly outnumbered. Foggarty made a grab at his ear but he ducked.

'Running away are yer – yer frit yer cowardly polliwog. His father's in gaol – he's a felon,' he sneered. There was a loud guffaw from behind. Charley, stung by these words picked up a stone.

'Yer wry-faced priggers!' He spat out the words as he flung it with all his might. Foggarty put his hand to his head where a trickle of blood was running down.

'Right! Let's teach the game-cock a lesson boys!' The next thing Charley knew he was being flung aloft by a sea of arms. He struggled, kicked and yelled but with whoops and shouts that made the echoes ring, they trundled him along and dumped him as hard as they could in a patch of brambles and stinging nettles.

It seemed to Charley he was being lashed by swords. He was numb from shock and pain. He vaguely heard them going off like yelling devils. Somehow he managed to scramble out. He folded his arms round his body. It was worse than being stung by a thousand bees. He pressed his eyes tight together. In spite of himself, tears were rolling down his cheeks.

'Charley! Whatever have you been up to?'

Beth was appalled at the sight of him when he finally reached home.

'I fell in some brambles.'

'Thou art not telling me the truth, Charley.' She looked hard at him – so he had to tell the whole story.

She bathed his stings and deep scratches with moss dipped in garlic water and then put on some of Martha's comfrey ointment to soothe and heal them.

'I wish thee would not fall foul of that Faulk Foggarty, Charley,' she said as she sat mending his torn shirt and hose.

'Thee knowest his father's just waiting for any excuse to turn us out of this cottage.'

'I'll have some work for thee to do tomorrow,' said John. 'that will keep thee out of mischief.'

'What sort of work?' Charley wailed, still suffering from his wounds.

'I'll tell thee in the morning,' was John's reply.

August had been a very dry month, and the rainwater well at the back of their cottage was almost empty. Slimy black sediment lay at the bottom, so John decided to go down and clean it out before the next rains came. In the meantime they would have to fetch their water, either from Slade Brook or the spring in Kettering Road.

The following morning, John hooked a rope ladder on to the top of the well, and descended with a leather bucket tied to a long cord. At this moment Piers arrived.

'I'm not in friends with thee,' said Charley sulkily. 'Thou ran off yesterday and left me to face Faulk Foggarty alone.'

'If you'd had any sense you'd ha' run off too. It's best not to face him. He's twice as big as we are and we'd always get the worst of it.'

'I thought friends had to stick together.' Charley was still sulky. 'Anyway I can't go out with you this morning.'

'Hey, what's to do up there?' came John's hollow voice from the depths of the well. 'Stop all the talking – I want some help. Pull up this bucket and throw the sludge onto the garden.'

'I'll help you,' Piers volunteered, to get in Charley's good books again. 'My, 'tis plaguey deep down there,' he said peering into the well.

So the two of them tugged at the rope, gradually easing up the heavy bucket and tipping it where John had told them, before dropping it down to him again. This went on for some time until their arms and backs and legs began to ache and Charley's freckled face got redder as he struggled and tugged.

'Ugh! This is smelly stuff!' was Pier's breathless comment.

'Almost the last bucket!' came John's muffled and echoing voice.

'Heave heave, heave, pull,' shouted the boys as together they tugged at the rope.

Suddenly it was light – the weight had gone. There was a sickening, squelching sound at the bottom and a yell from John.

The boys gasped and looked at each other, and then burst into laughter, as slowly he emerged, covered from head to foot with smelly, black sludge.

'Tripehounds thou art! Why did thou not hold the rope tightly?' he shouted as he spat and spluttered. Beth emerged at that moment.

'God bless my soul!' she exclaimed. 'Take a bucket each and fetch some water from Slade Brook!'

Two were by no means enough and they had to go many times before John and his clothes were fit to go indoors.

'Tripehounds thou art! Why did thou not hold the rope tightly?' John shouted as he spat and spluttered. 'God bless my soul!' Beth exclaimed. 'Take a bucket and fetch some water from Slade Brook!'

CHAPTER

12

Harvest time . . . gleaning.
The mill
Mistress Ragford's illness. John rides to Northampton to fetch Dr Cogan.

One bright morning, bread and cheese wrapped in a kerchief, Beth and Charley set off to go gleaning.

The early September days were warm and sunny but the mornings and evenings had a nip in the air and whisps of mist lingered over Slade Brook well after sunrise.

Farmer Thacker's labourers had reaped the oats and barley in August and now the ripe wheat stood high, swaying in the breeze with a sound like the sea on the shore, and cutting had begun. The reapers, at work from early dawn, could be seen plodding wearily home, their scythes in one hand and dead rabbits tied together in the other. Village boys had been with them all day, pouncing on the rabbits as they fled from the sweeping blades, and killing them with a blow of the hand.

'The field-mice and voles will have to find fresh homes,' said Piers as he and Charley watched.

'The stoats and weasels will get them, the bloodthirsty things,' said Charley.

Beth and Martha were still busy out of doors, for this was harvest time, a time of stocking up for the Winter. Over on the common were luscious ripe blackberries, big juicy ones, harbouring drunken wasps. If Charley and Sammy were there helping, they enjoyed getting a handful of the berries and slapping them into their mouths leaving purple stains all round, or, in the woods, gathering hazel nuts in their brown cups, cracking them and crunching happily on the milky kernels. It was a not wise to delay the nut collecting too long or the mice and squirrels would have added them to their Winter store. There was great excitement for Charley and Sammy when they could pounce on mushrooms hiding in the green 'fairy rings' and fill their basket to overflowing. Martha was delighted when she came across the bristly heads of teasel. They were just what she wanted for smoothing out the wool before she did her spinning.

One bright morning, bread and cheese wrapped in a kerchief, Beth and Charley set off to go gleaning. Once the corn had been cut and cleared, the leavings were for the taking. As they crossed the hump-back bridge over Slade Brook, came the call of 'Crek-rek-rek.'

'Moorhens,' said Charley, peering over the bridge to watch them bobbing and dipping in the sedges, making a silver ripple in the deep green water.

A pig was rootling by the roadside as they went along.

'Look!' said Charley, 'he's eating with his head to the wind, that means it will be a fine day.'

'How do you know?' asked Beth.

'Because old Hatchet at the farm told me. If an animal crops with its tail to the wind it's going to rain.'

Beth laughed. 'Dr Ragford says you'll make a good naturalist whatever that is; I just wish you were good at reading, writing and accounts.'

'I am,' persisted Charley, 'at least I'm getting better.'

As they went along, a deafening noise came from a group of tall elms, a chattering, raucous noise that clawed at their ears. Charley banged his hands together and suddenly there was silence as a black cloud of starlings blew off like living leaves and disappeared.

All day they worked, through the hot mid-day sun and on into the evening, backs bent in the stubble – Charley complaining it prickled through his hosen. They stopped once to have a bite to eat and a drink of ale, and chewed a handful of ripe corn rubbed from the ear. All over the field, women from the village were working, their kirtles tucked up showing their red stammel petticoats underneath. Beth took pity on an old woman who reminded her of 'Mother' Stephens, and gave her some of her gleanings. Small, frightened creatures, field mice, voles and birds were gleaning what they could in their own way.

By sundown, when deep shadows stole across the stubble, the gleaners had the wheat stalks tied in bundles, as much as they could carry on their bent backs. A sudden wind blew up with the setting sun, and great storm clouds filled the sky. Before long the rain was sheeting down, turning the dusty ruts to mud. Beth was gasping for breath as she fought her way home through the wind and rain, Charley struggling in the rear. They were soaked as they cast off their burdens into the barn outside.

'So much for your pig, rootling with his head to the wind,' said Beth, pulling off her wet clothes.

'But it has been fine all day,' Charley persisted.

Next day, all three of them got to work. Taking a handful of stalks at a time, they banged the ears onto a stone slab out at the back. Then using their fire bellows gently, they puffed the chaff away. By the time it was all finished, there was nearly a

The stately old mill, mounted on it's heavy swivelling post, stood atop of Windmill Hill.

sack full and John put it onto their little hand cart and he and Charley took it to the miller. The stately old mill, mounted on its heavy swivelling post, stood atop of Windmill Hill (on the way out of the village towards Kettering) as many others stood in the villages round about. Perched on the highest hills, Charley wondered if they ever talked to each other across the fields and commons as they twisted and turned and waved their arms around.

John pulled the sack (marked so that he would know it) up the ricketty steps. Inside there was a creaking and groaning as if all the rusty wheels and chains in the world were grinding, and the whole mill seemed to be aching with painful old age. Miller Browne came backwards down his ricketty ladders. From head to toe he was white, like the cobwebs that hung everywhere, dusty with flour.

'I'll do me best fo' yer,' was his answer to John's request. 'It's a lot I got ter do just now – come back day arter tomorrow.'

The sun was shining and as they stepped outside; the mill's arms flung round, passing their great shadows over them.

'He ought to be called Miller White not Browne,' said Charley as they trundled the cart back home again. 'His hair is white, and his hands and clothes and shoen are white. I wonder if he still looks white when he goes to Church on Sundays.'

Meanwhile Beth had been amusing herself making corn dollies from the stalks and had hung them up in the house. 'They're the spirits of the corn and will bring a good harvest next year. I think one has to be buried in the corn field, but perhaps the reapers did that,' she said putting the finishing touches to the last one.

A big red harvest moon hung in the sky as Beth climbed into bed that night. She saw it through a tangle of wind-swept branches like straggly hair across a face, and it somehow reminded her of Mother Stephens, as Watercress Willy called her. She had to admit to herself that her father had been right when he said all their needs would be supplied. 'But,' she added, half aloud, 'we've had to work hard too. Perhaps we haven't been thankful enough for all the good things that have happened to us. I must remember to thank the Lord for them when I say my prayer this night.'

October approached and the swallows had gone, but there was still a mellow warmness in the air. Some early morning frost had dyed the oaks a deeper bronze, splashed the elms with pale yellow, turned the beeches to orange, the sycamores to scarlet and dressed the silver birch, the 'dainty lady of the woods', in a gown of gold.

John was pleased with his job at the Crown. It satisfied two of his loves, animals and reading. He loved to hear the stamp of hooves on the stable floor, the whinnying, the swish of hay, the clatter of wooden buckets and the rhythmic crunch of the oats. He liked to get a tit-bit from Anna-in-the kitchen, and feel their wrinkling, velvety noses as they took it from his flat hand. He loved the warm smell of their coats as he brushed them down. Even the smell of manure had a kind of fascination about it. He was watching them one day, sucking the water he had just brought, when Owen Ragford came hurrying into the stable yard. He looked worried and agitated, which was quite unlike him.

'Is Ostler Amos around!' he called.

'I am here sir!' and he came out from one of the stables. 'Anything I can do for ye - want the hire of a horse sir?'

'I want one of your men Amos, a good reliable one, who will ride to Northampton for me - it is very urgent.'

'I'll go Dr Ragford, right willingly.' John stepped forward. 'That is if Amos can spare me.' Amos nodded and Owen drew John aside.

'This is very urgent and very important,' he said hastily, 'but I know I can trust you. My wife has suddenly taken ill and my old friend Eliezer Cogan, the apothecary, is on a visit to friends in Northampton. I want you to ride there with all speed and tell him he must come at once. See here is the address and a note I have written to him.'

John quickly prepared a swift horse he knew he could trust. 'Ride hard my boy, for it is a matter of life and death I fear.'

'That I will sir,' and he set off at once, pausing only on his way out of the village to tell Beth where he was going, and that having delivered his message, he would stay the night with Martha's brother if he could, and visit their father on the morrow. Beth packed him some bread and cheese in a kerchief and wished him God-speed.

The horse, Old Faithful, was one John knew and loved. He asked her now to be swift and she galloped hard, with the jingle of harness and the ring of hooves on the roadway, or left her prints deep in the soft turf when they cut off across the commons. Her mane spread loose over the rippling muscles of her neck and her silky chestnut coat, the strong, stiff hairs of her sweeping tail dancing up and down to the rhythm of the gallop.

At home Beth was worried. 'Poor Marie,' she thought, 'I wonder if there is ought I could do to help.' But when she

'Ride hard my boy for it is a matter of life and death I fear.'

went to the house, the servant who answered her knock, shook her head sadly, and as she closed the door, she could see her eyes were red with weeping.

'Pray the Good Lord, 'tis not the plague,' she thought as she made her way back again.

Martha called that evening, going home from the Manor, with some venison pasty and half a fruit pie for them. Beth spoke to her of Mistress Ragford's illness and Martha promised to bring her some rosemary and lavender to hang in the house on the morrow. 'Tis of the greatest good to

The horse, Old Faithful, was one John knew and loved. He asked her now to be swift, and she galloped hard with a jingle of harness and the ring of hooves on the roadway.

ward off the pestilence should it strike in the village,' she said.

After some searching, John found Doctor Cogan, the apothecary, at the house Owen had indicated. He read the note and promised to ride back immediately even though the day was far spent. John then went on to Martha's brother who welcomed him and said that he too was of the Puritan faith and very sympathetic to his father. 'Although I have it not in my heart to go to prison,' he confessed.

Visiting his father in gaol, the next day, he was glad to see him looking better than he had expected, for they had learned from Martha about the gaol fever. He was anxious about them all and wanted to be back to his shoemaking, but was still determined he would defy the law by preaching, holding prayer meetings and worshipping God in his own way. John told him what they had all been doing and about the weekly new's-sheet at the Crown Inn.

'I think now this Cromwell has charge of the government, he may well pass a law in the Parliament House to give people like thee, father, who will not conform to the church, freedom to worship as they think fit.'

'Ah, would thou art right,' Nathaniel replied, 'but the wheels of government grind slow, like the wheels of the old post-mill – extremely slow. We can but hope and pray. Look after Beth and young Charley and God be with thee all my boy.'

'And with thee too father,' said John as he took his leave.

The apothecary's potion, whatever it was, seemed to have helped Mistress Ragford to recover, but it was several weeks before Beth was again asked to go and read to her, and even then she looked tired and pale as she sat wrapped up in her high-backed chair, and asked that she did not stay too long. So Beth read for a while, and then as Marie seemed to fall asleep, she tiptoed out, down the stairs and into the street, closing the outer door softly behind her. As she did so and turned, she came face to face with Owen. There was a smile in his eyes now as he said, 'We're glad to see you again Beth.'

She walked home with a lighter heart now that she was sure Mistress Ragford would soon be fully recovered and hoped beyond all things that she would not still be thinking of going back to France. The upper branches of the trees showed bare against the sky, and leaves, red, brown, silver and gold, were falling, deep and rustling under foot, as she walked down Kettering Road and turned into Meadow Lane.

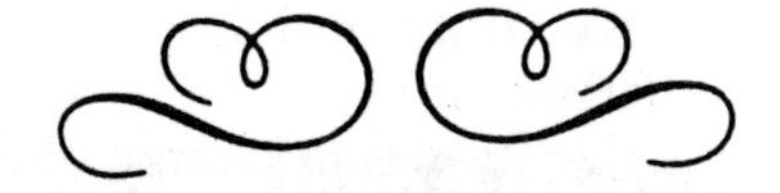

CHAPTER

13

Charley loses the 'Hidey' Box.
Martha and Sammy go to Northampton again.
Beth is scared.

Beth jumped up with a scream and rushed to bolt the door, for she was sure the Devil himself was outside.

As October crept on and the days became chillier, John realized one morning that their Winter stock of fuel was too low. 'It ought to be piled high up along the cottage wall,' he said. So whenever they could, they set off to the woods, to collect as much as possible before the weather broke. There were plenty of fallen branches that could be dragged home for John to saw into logs.

If Charley went with Piers however, *their* chief interest was in things to eat, berries or nuts, or in 'finds' for their collections. 'I'm looking for snails, toads and frogs,' Charley announced one day as they set off with cords to tie the faggots and two rush baskets for cones and smaller kindling.

'They go to sleep in the Winter and I'm going to keep some in a box.'

'Where?' asked Piers.

'I don't know, but it will have to be somewhere Beth won't find them, or she'll throw them away.'

'You'll have a job to hide anything from Beth,' Piers laughed. 'If she's like my mother, she knows everything I do before I do it, and says, Don't".'

A sort of mocking laugh came through the wood. 'Hear that?' Piers stopped to listen.

'Yes, it's a green woodpecker,' Charley replied.

'Coo-coo-ooo, Coo-coo-ooo, came the soft voice of a wood pigeon, high up in an ash tree.

Plodding along the mossy woodland path, they surprised a squirrel enjoying his feast of beech mast, and he scampered away up the trunk. It was a mildish day and clouds of gnats were dancing in the air, and honey-bees, wasps and bluebottles were on the ivys. The Autumn gales had stripped the trees so the two boys leapt into deep beds of fallen leaves, and with whoops and shouts, flung them high in the air and great armfuls at each other, in sheer delight.

Charley stopped and bent down. 'Got him!' he cried triumphantly, as with two handfuls of leaves he picked up something carefully and popped it into the basket.

'What's that?' Piers was interested.

'A hedgehog,' said Charley, 'It's getting sleepy.'

'Augh, they're prickly, fleay things. I'll look in hollow tree trunks and bark ridges for moths and butterflies and caterpillars and chrysalises.' He cautiously lifted some nettle leaves and picked off a 'woolly bear', which curled to a ball in his hand. 'That's the Tiger Moth's caterpillar,' he explained.

'I know that,' said Charley disdainfully.

'I bet you never found a Death's Head,' Piers boasted. Charley had to admit he had not. 'I found one last Autumn. It had a skull mark on its head and when I touched it, it squeaked like a mouse. I'd love to find one of its caterpillars – they're huge with all yellow, green and violet stripes.'

But Charley was not listening. He was collecting his own assortment. He lifted a rotten tree stump with a brown pan-cake fungus growing out of it, and underneath was a sleepy green toad all rough and nobbly.

'Eer – ugly thing – you're not going to take that!' Piers opened his eyes wide as Charley popped it in with the hedgehog, along with some beetles and snails.

'Who says I'm not?' Then suddenly realizing it was for firewood they had come, and that the light in the coppice was fading,' he said, 'I'd better get some more faggots before it gets too dark,' and they hastily bent their backs to work and gathered frantically for a time, putting it into piles. Then, tying it together, they dragged it along, kicking great soft puff-balls with their feet, and jumping on the 'candle-snuff' fungi to see the brown 'smoke' come out. Charley dropped the sticks out at the back and hid his 'finds' in an old leather bucket.

Next morning Beth took a look at the small pile. 'Thee didst not get much wood yesterday,' she commented.

'We had to go farther afield and it took longer,' was Charley's excuse.

There was no school this day and in the middle of the morning he was pleased to see Beth go off with her shopping basket. He had been hoping for an opportunity to hide his 'finds'. As soon as she was safely out of the way, he got an old box from his father's workshed, lined it with grass, and put in the snails, beetles, caterpillars and chrysalises, deciding that after all he would take the toad and hedgehog back and put them in his secret den in the wood, the place where he and Sammy had hidden from Faulk Foggarty and his gang. They would be safe there and he could go and look at them whenever he wanted.

'Now where can I hide this box?' he wondered looking round. Then he had an idea. 'I know, on top of the partition between the two bedrooms.' Nobody, not even Beth, ever looks up there – it's all cobwebby.' Climbing onto the bed and standing on tiptoe, he ran his fingers along the ledge to find a good place, for in some parts it was wider than others.

To his surprise, another box was already there. This was interesting. He managed to slide it off and shook it. Something fairly heavy was inside that rattled, but try as he might, nothing would move the lid. Then he discovered 'N. PONDER' engraved in the wood on the underneath side. 'Must be father's,' he thought. 'But why is it up on that ledge?' Here was a mystery and Charley loved mysteries. His thumbs and fingers went to work, but pulling hard, he dropped it with a bang on the floor.

So engrossed had he been, that he did not realise Beth was back until he heard her voice calling him. There was no time to replace it, she had heard the bump and was coming up. He was sure to be chastised.

He looked round quickly. The window was slightly open, so he dropped it out and it fell into a bush below. He was going to throw out his own box too, but she was already at the top of the stair. 'Whatever art thou doing Charley? I hope thou art not bringing any more of thy 'finds' up here.' And then she spotted it. 'I knew thou wert up to something. Now what's in that box on the bed?'

'There's only some caterpillars, a butterfly and a few snails,' Charley pleaded. 'They will sleep all the Winter.'

'Not up here they won't.' Beth was quite adamant. 'Take them out at the back somewhere or get rid of them.'

Charley argued no further, for he was anxious to get down and hide the other box in a safer place. Every time he tried to go to it however, Beth seemed to be around. 'I'll take it to my secret place in the wood,' he thought. 'I can have a better look there and perhaps get it open.'

Beth always thought it was best to keep Charley busy so it was late in the afternoon, before he slung the big rush basket over his shoulder and shouted he was off to collect some fuel. She came to the door as he was setting out, surprised he was going unasked. Seeing some leaves at the bottom of the basket, she said, 'What hast thou there Charley?'

'I'm taking my finds" back to the wood,' he replied. 'Thee said I had to get rid of them.'

'I don't mind if thee keeps them – but not in the house.'

'But there's a toad as well, and a hedgehog, and Piers says they're full of fleas.'

'And so they are,' Beth pulled a face. 'Go and get rid of them for goodness sake – and don't keep looking for things – curiosity killed the cat you know.'

Charley skipped off, glad that he had got away. Reaching his hiding place in the wood, he crawled through a tunnel of undergrowth and brambles and came out into a mossy space with the hollow tree in the middle of it. Here he could have another go at the box without fear of interruption. He shook it from side to side, pulled and wriggled.

After some time however, having no luck, he gave it up and decided he had better take it home and put it back on the ledge at the first opportunity. For the time being he laid it in the hollow tree along with the hedgehog and toad, covered them all with dead leaves, and went off to collect some wood.

Today he did have to go farther afield than usual to get his basket full and it took longer than he expected, for there was no Sammy or Piers to help. It seemed to grow dark quickly under the trees. As he went back towards his hiding place, he thought he heard the snapping of twigs. Pausing to listen, he heard no more, so he crawled through the tunnel in the half light and put his hand into the hollow trunk. The hedgehog was there. The toad was there – but where was the box? Perhaps he had put in in a slightly different place. It was difficult to see. It must be somewhere there. He felt all round. Nothing. 'I'll have to go home now,' he decided. 'I'll come back tomorrow when it's light.'

Next day however, brought no more success – the box was certainly not there. Nobody could have taken it, he argued to himself, for nobody knew of his hiding place, not even Piers.

Yes, somebody did – Sammy – he was the only one he had ever taken there when they hid from Faulk Foggarty. Sammy often wandered in the wood and might have been able to find it again. If he had found the box, he would think it was just something to play with. 'I must take him back there, and somehow make him understand it was *my* box – which will be difficult,' he thought.

But his hopes were dashed. When he got home, Martha and Sammy were there. She was going to Northampton immediately she said, for her brother's wife had died, leaving him with three small children to look after. 'Oh dear,' he thought, 'now it will be ages before I can get anything out of Sammy.' But Charley was not one to worry unduly. 'Oh well,' he thought, 'it's only an old box anyway. It's probably been there for a hundred years, so nobody will miss it. But I should have liked to know what was inside.'

Beth was having a last chat with Martha and looked unhappy. 'When ever shall we see thee again?' she said gloomily.

'Be of good cheer Beth, it won't be too long I hope – just till my brother can get someone to look after his house and the children. Let us see, today is the last of October – I promise you I will be back for Christmas at any rate, and we will spend it together.'

'And we'll go up to Sweetbriar Cottage now and again and see that everything is all right,' said Beth.

John, working late at the Crown that evening, saw Martha and Sammy onto the stage wagon as it came through and bade them God-speed.

Charley, the box almost forgotten, had gone to Pier's house, and Beth sat all alone, looking at the black charred sticks on the hearth and the red glow of the dying embers in the ash. Her thoughts were not very cheerful. How long would it be before they saw Martha again? Tomorrow would be November – another Winter coming. She recalled the last one with its bitter weather and its chilblains. And their father – he would have to face at least part of it in that ice cold gaol. Would they be able to manage till he came home? There was one thing to be thankful for. By their work and thrift during the Summer and Autumn, they had made sure there was enough money in the 'Hidey' Box to pay the rent when Bailiff Foggarty came in December.

A slight noise made her turn quickly. Looking in at the window were two gleaming eyes, a nose and a wide open, grinning mouth with long fang-like teeth. She had been so deep in thought, sitting there in the darkness, that this sudden apparition thoroughly startled her and she jumped up with a scream

Beth sat all alone looking at the black charred sticks on the hearth and the red glow of the dying embers in the ash. Her thoughts were not very cheerful.

and rushed to bolt the door, for she was sure the Devil himself was outside. And then there was a banging and a shouting and hilarious laughter.

'Beth! Beth!' The Devil was calling her by name – but no, it was not the Devil's voice, but one she knew well. She unbarred the door and peeped out. 'It's only us Beth,' laughed Charley, 'me and Piers. Did thee forget, it's Halloween? Pier's father gave us a turnip to hollow out and we put a lighted dip inside to fright away witches and devils, for they fly around this night.'

'I don't know about witches and devils, but thee scared the life out of me!' Beth grumbled, as Charley and Piers dashed off to frighten someone else.

She had been anxious about the coming months, but that word 'WITCHES' reminded her of 'Mother' Stephens and what she had said to her. 'I won't cross bridges before I come to them and I'll leave tomorrow to look after itself.'

CHAPTER

14

John's arm is broken.
'Woolly' has to go back.
Charley falls ill.
John becomes Dr. Logan's apprentice.

Old 'Hatchett' sat there smoking his upturned pipe. With a whack on Woolly's fat sides, he sent him to join the flock.

They had not noticed him all Summer, but as the colder weather came, a robin hopped around the house. He was on the window ledge almost before daybreak, standing on his thin little legs, his breast the colour of an Autumn leaf, bobbing, flicking his wings and calling, 'Tic-tic,' as he turned his head from side to side. When Beth threw out a crumb or two, he would make a quick dive and then vanish. She shivered as she came back one morning from feeding him. ' 'Tis raw cold outside,' she said, 'to be sure we'll soon have snow.'

'Old Hatchet and his weather lore isn't always right,' said Beth, remembering gleaning day when it was supposed to be fine. As John walked up Kettering Road on his way to The Crown, cap pulled well on his head and muffler round his neck and mouth, the cottages and trees stood like shrouded ghosts and loomed up at him out of the mist as he passed. November had come indeed.

In the stable yard, the patient horses were waiting for oats and hay, their breath rising like smoke in the frosty air, while all round, bold tits, squabbling sparrows and sooty male blackbirds with their dusky wives, gathered for what they could glean. The Inn was unusually busy that morning. The courtyard rang with the stamp and clatter of hooves on the cobble stones, and the voices of the ostlers mingled with the post-boys as they shouted out the latest news from London and other cities to the North. 'There's a-bin a hold-up by Whittlebury Forest,' cried one. 'Seven men attacked the guard of the stage-wagon from Northampton to Oxford. The guard shot three o' the highwaymen dead with his blunder-bus afore he was killed at his post!' This was one of the usual hazards of the road and nobody seemed unduly surprised.

Fresh relays of horses were in demand for the wealthy family coaches, for the stage-wagons, for the Government Messengers riding up and down the country, and for locals who wanted a mount for journeys that were too far on foot. About the middle of the morning, Owen Ragford came to the stables. He often hired a horse and he and Amos were good friends.

'John, fetch old Sorrel for Dr Ragford – he gets on well with him,' he called.

'Right thee are sir,' John answered, 'I'll have him ready

before thou can say, 'Oliver Cromwell!'

Old Sorrel was noted for being pleasant tempered, but today something must have been wrong, for as John went to back him out of the stable, he was restless and stamped and fidgeted, whinnying and snorting as he flung up his head and tossed a tangle of black mane.

There he was, standing on his thin little legs, his breast the colour of an Autumn leaf, flicking his wings and calling, 'Tic-tic'.

'Come on, old one.' John gave his flank a gentle pat. Suddenly his leg kicked back. John gave a sharp cry of pain which brought Owen and the ostler to see what was amiss. He was in obvious distress, holding one arm with the other.

Owen realized immediately what had happened. 'Come with me quickly,' he said, 'to my friend Dr Cogan, the apothecary, it looks to me as though it is broken.'

John knew Eliezer Cogan well. He was often called in by Amos to attend a sick horse, for he treated animals as well as people. His shop, with its mixture of herb smells, its bottles and jars, its pestles and mortars, its books and scales and countless small drawers labled with Latin names, was not far away in Tresham Street. John saw it but hazily, in considerable pain, as the Doctor set and bandaged his broken arm.

When Beth came home an hour or so later, she found him white-faced, with his arm bound up, being given some water by Owen Ragford. She was shocked and frightened. 'Don't worry too much, your brother has had an accident with one of the horses. His arm is broken, but my good friend the apothecary, has set it for him and given him a potion to help with the pain. What he has to do now is take care for a time till it knits together.'

'Oh poor John,' said Beth. 'Does it hurt thee very much?'

John gave a wry smile.

'I think I may survive,' he said. 'I was lucky Dr Ragford was there and that I could go straight to the apothecary.'

'If thee'll wait a minute sir, I'll fetch some money to pay him.'

'My dear Beth, Dr Cogan says you owe him nothing and he will see John again in a month.'

'A month sir?' Beth's anxious face looked up at him.

'I'm afraid it will take longer than that before it is fully healed and he can do his job again. I'll leave you now with, I am sure, a very capable nurse.' And Owen smiled at them, wriggling his beard and moustaches in that funny way Beth had grown to know so well. 'I will call tomorrow to see how you are.' He strode out, shutting the door behind him.

Beth looked at John lying on their father's settle.

'Whatever shall we do now?' she said in despair.

'We'll manage somehow. 'But John did not feel as cheerful

'Oh poor John,' said Beth, 'Does it hurt thee very much?'

as he tried to sound.

'Thou hast thy reading job with Mistress Ragford and we have *some* spare money in the 'Hidey' Box. Before long I'll be able to chop the wood and fetch the buckets of water at any rate.'

'With one hand, and that thy left?' Beth questioned. 'Our Charley will have to bestir himself and do some of thy tasks. How I wish Martha was here.'

Owen called on them next day as he had promised. 'I see

your patient is doing very well,' he smiled, for although John's arm was very swollen and painful, his face was a better colour and he was a little more cheerful.

'Amos wants to see you when you can go up to the Crown,' he continued. 'My wife sends her condolences John, and hopes to see *you* tomorrow Beth.'

Accordingly, the next day, they walked up together, John going to the Inn and Beth to the Ragford's. Mine Host at the Crown was sorry about the accident.

'I'll pay your wage for this week,' he said, 'but after that, not until you are working again. If however, you come and read the news-sheet as usual, I'll give you something for that.' This cheered John considerably, and Beth too when she heard it.

It got toward the end of November. Woolly, was now a fat, full-grown lamb and a family pet, eating the grass, following them around and walking in and out of the house like a dog. 'I'd better take him back to the farm,' said John. 'There won't be enough food for him here in the Winter.' This upset Charley.

'But he'll be happier back with all the others,' Beth consoled him.

So one morning John set out for Three Chimneys with Woolly in tow. Ploughmen were plodding up and down the tawny acres behind their teams of horses and on the broken soil a swarm of jackdaws, rooks, crows and plovers foraged for food. As he neared the farm he could see in the distance, some of the shepherds already preparing for the next early lambs. Sheep were standing around and he found Old Hatchet taking fodder to their troughs. 'If it ain't young Ponder,' he said, taking out his upturned pipe and spitting. He looked at John's bandaged arm and heard the story of how it happened. 'That's working at yer fancy places. Thought yer were too good fer us I imagine. My old mother used ter say knit-bone were good fer broken bones – grows down by the brook in ditches, if there's any about now.' And with a whack on Woolly's fat sides, he sent him to join the flock.

As John passed the kitchen door of the farmhouse, there was a delicious smell of newly baked bread. Goodwife Thacker came out at that moment and seeing him and his bandaged arm, fetched him a drink of ale and a fresh loaf and a piece of bacon to take home with him. He told her about Woolly.

'You've spoiled him,' she laughed. 'He'll think he's a dog now and want to wander in and out of the kitchen as he pleases.'

John walked home in the evening sunlight.

'JOHN PONDER!' he shouted to the Echo Barn across the fields, and smiled as 'John Ponder!' came the echoing reply. The trees were bare now and their black branches were etched against rose-tinted clouds and a turquoise sky.

'Is our Charley not in yet? He should be by now,' he remarked as he sat down by the fire. He peered under the table – one of Charley's favourite places.

'Yes, he's in,' said Beth, 'but he said he felt sick and did not want any supper, so I sent him up to bed.'

'There must be something wrong if Charley doesn't want his food – leave him alone, perhaps he will be better in the morning,' John replied. Smoke from the rush candles hung about the room in a haze as they ate the loaf Goodwife Thacker had given them with cheese and onion. It was a chilly night and Beth threw some more kindling on the fire as John took down their father's Bible and they each chose a passage to read aloud before they climbed up to bed. Charley seemed to be asleep.

It must have been sometime in the middle of the night when they were awakened by a terrific noise. Beth jumped out of bed and John from his. It was Charley, screaming and shouting. 'They're coming for me! Don't let them get me . . . don't let them . . . they're under the bed! I didn't mean to do it . . . I'll find it . . . it's Sammy . . . go and get him. . . .'

'There, there, Charley, what ails thee? Come and lie down and go to sleep – thou wert having a bad dream.'

He had calmed down a little and Beth tucked him into bed again, but he was shaking all over, shivering and still wailing, 'Don't let them get me!'

'Nobody's going to get thee Charley,' she said soothingly. 'Who would be anyway?'

'The hobgoblins and foul fiends. They came in the window and made faces at me and they're all green with long arms and prickles and big lumps and they're going to get me and lock me up!' Beth noticed he was burning hot and had no idea what he was saying. She thought of Maria and her illness and had not others in the village had the sickness also?

She hardly dared to express her fear – was it the Plague? She dropped to her knees by the bedside. 'Dear Lord,' she murmured, 'father says we can talk to Thee as a friend – do not visit us with the pestilence I beseech Thee.' Groping her way downstairs, she fetched some water from the trough outside. She gave him a drink and wrung out a cloth, putting it on to his burning forehead. He was still tossing and turning.

'The foul fiends . . . and big green toads . . . they said I stole it. I didn't, I didn't I didn't!'

'Of course you didn't, now go to sleep chicken.' And Beth wrung the cloth out again and put it on his head.

Presently he fell into an uneasy slumber.

'Get into bed John and I'll stay with him for a while.' It was a stormy night and a tree outside creaked and groaned in the wind.

She sat on the bare boards by his bed, her head resting against it. He was still restless and crying out from time to time, but at last she must have fallen asleep herself.

It was a dull wild morning when Beth woke, stiff and cold. Charley seemed to be half awake but there was no look of recognition on his face when she spoke to him. He was still burning hot, throwing his arms about and pulling at the bed covers which were all awry from his feverish tossings.

A box had fallen out from it on to the floor, a little broken box she had seen many times in her father's workshop. She picked it up and opened it. Inside were three snails, a 'woolly bear' caterpillar, a chrysalis and a butterfly with folded wings. She looked from them to Charley still in a nightmarish half sleep, still tossing and turning, still feverishly hot. Beth did not often weep, but at this moment she fell on her knees by the bedside. 'Charley, Charley,' she cried softly, 'do, do get better – please do. You can keep anything in the house you want and I won't grumble;' and she buried her red-gold hair in the bed clothes.

John, weary from his own pain, roused himself and prepared to get up. For the next week Beth was so occupied with Charley, that he had to manage as best he could. Night after night she sat by his bed, bathing his forehead and giving him drinks. John remembered their father used to make them an infusion of yarrow leaves for feverish colds, and he managed to find a few late plants on Underwood Common. Beth also made some mutton broth and lemon balm, and remembering what Martha had told her, spread the floor with dried thyme and lavender to make the room smell fresh.

Whether it was the yarrow tea or the mutton broth, or just that the fever had run its course, Charley gradually began to improve, until, pale and weak, he was able to get down the stairs and wrapped up, sit by the fire.

They were a spent and weary little band who sat by the embers of an evening. Beth felt they had come to one of Mother Stephen's 'bridges' and were having a struggle to cross it. 'We haven't much for supper,' said John one night as he peered into the old iron pot hanging over the fire. 'It's half empty.'

'Not half empty,' said Beth cheerfully, 'It's half full!'

She bustled about. 'It won't be too long now before father can come home, and Martha too, if you remember, promised to be back by Christmas.'

When John went to see Eliezer Cogan, the good old physician smiled and said his arm was doing well. 'Just take care for a time,' he said, 'and give it a chance to heal. You are young and strong – it shouldn't take too long.'

At this moment Owen Ragford came into the apothecary's shop, stocked with its pungent herbs, oils and potions. 'And how's that arm of yours, John?' he inquired.

'Dr Cogan says it is doing well and will soon be healed,' he replied.

'Good, now that's a fortunate thing,' he said turning to Eliezer, 'you were saying but yesterday you were getting older and needed an apprentice to help you. Here is the very one! He can read and write and is quick and willing. To be sure he doesn't know Latin, but he'll soon learn. He has worked with animals and horses and can help you with them, and as for your infusions and potions and nostrums and douches and leeches and cuppings and blisterings and blood lettings – breathing a vein do you call it? – and all your other mysteries, he'll be mixing and administering them all in no time.'

Dr Cogan smiled. He turned to John. 'You must be prepared to ride abroad in the wind and all weathers to tend man and beast. It will need every dram of your ability lad, and as

'Now that's a fortunate thing,' said Owen, 'you were saying but yesterday you were getting older and needed an apprentice to help you. Here is the very one!'

much active sympathy as you are capable of.'

'He has plenty of that,' Owen assured him. 'He is a country lad bred and born, and although the family are Puritans and do not attend church, they are truly Christian and have a strong belief in God.'

Eliezer looked hard at him. 'I believe you're right,' he said quietly. 'When I am in London, I believe in the Devil, but when I am in the country, I believe in God.'

By the nodding and smiling of the two men and their privately whispered words, John could see they thought he would be the right choice, but for his part he was fearful of his ability to do such a difficult job. He had always thought of the apothecary, with all his learning, as far above anything he could ever achieve, but when he expressed his doubts, Owen's reply was, 'Everyone has to learn, and in learning, all must begin from the bottom. A dozen years or so with Dr Cogan, and we shall have two able physicians in Rowell.'

So it was decided that he should come to the apothecary's shop as soon as possible and begin to learn some of the mysteries of his art.

John walked home, whistling happily that day, dodging a noisy crowd of youths playing football in the street. He could, see in imagination, a sign over the shop in Tresham Street:

ELIEZER COGAN and JOHN PONDER
APOTHECARIES

Pestle
and Mortar
APOTHECARY
Foxglove or Digitalis
Deadly Nightshade or Belladonna.

CHAPTER

15

A chapter of surprises as Christmas Day comes.

Beth was determined their little cottage should be bright and gay in its own fashion.

November crept on into December and December towards Christmastide.

John's arm was much improved and he was enjoying his first weeks with Dr Cogan. Charley was almost back to his usual hungry self, while Beth was struggling to finish the three mufflers on her sticken pins. She wanted to make a present for Martha, and Mistress Ragford suggested a pomander ball. She gave her an orange, some cloves and cinnamon and a pretty ribbon to tie round it.

Snow had come with the Winter, not deep, but it rested on the roofs and window ledges like sugar icing. It lay along the tree branches, and in soft drifts among the reed beds by Slade Brook. It decorated the great cedars in the Manor park and wrapped the bushes in the formal garden by the house, in white drapery.

Beth could picture to herself what Christmas would be like at the great house – a blaze of lights everywhere and all the rooms hung with decorations of holly and ivy. Flames from the huge log fires would leap and spit, the dining table would groan with food, and the brightly coloured silks, satins, taffetas and velvets, would gleam and glint in the light of hundreds of candles as the dancers bowed and laughed, swirled and leapt around the Great Chamber to the music of the viols, the lutes, clarions, hautboys, and flageolets. Well, they could have their great banquets and balls, but she was determined their little cottage should also be bright and gay in its own fashion.

Their father, she knew, would not approve of decorations and celebrations, but, she argued to herself, Christmas was Christ's birthday and surely He would want them to rejoice and be glad in it.

She did hope Martha would be back as she had promised, but it got to the day before Christmas and still there was no sign of her. 'Come Charley,' Beth called, 'we will go to Slade Woods and get some greenery to decorate the house.' She put on her capa and chin clout, and Charley donned his jerkin and hose of kersey, with an old muffler round his neck and cap pulled well down over his ears. They blew their nails, flapped arms round their bodies and stamped their feet before picking up two big rush baskets.

Along the woodland path, Jack Frost had been before them

Beth and Charley fed the birds with left-over scraps as Wintery weather came.

with a magic brush, decorating every tree and thicket with lace and feathers of delicate white gossamer, and had thrown down a million sparkling diamonds that they crunched with abandon under their feet, singing as they went; at least Beth was -- Charley was whistling in his usual tuneless way. They filled the baskets with cones and wood, and with armfuls of greenery, holly and ivy, dragged it all home between them, their toes and fingers tingling with warmth.

Beth was gay, humming to herself as she kindled the fire, lit the dips, and with Charley's help, hung up the trimmings. They quite transformed their little room as the rush lights flickered on the leaves and berries. John had gone to Kettering Market to search for a chicken at a knock-down price as a special treat for their Christmas dinner. The decorations finished and the mess cleared up, Beth went to the window and peered out into the winter afternoon. How she wished she could see Martha and Sammy coming down the lane.

'John should be back by now,' she said. Charley detected an anxious note in her voice. 'I hope nothing can have happened to him. There are footpads around in Kettering.' Just then there was a banging at the door as though it was being hit with a heavy stick. It was flung open and in marched the burly figure of Bailiff Foggarty. With his broad-brimmed hat, cloak and jack-boots, he seemed to fill the little room. Charley fled under the table.

'Right, you Puritan Ponders – it's rent time!'

Beth was relieved it was only that, and managed a pleasant smile.

'If it will please thee sir to wait a minute, I'll go up and fetch it.'

He grunted, and while she was gone, he poked round the room with his stick, peering everywhere in his short-sighted way, and grunting again, sat down on the settle. Suddenly he spotted Charley under the table. 'What the devil are yer skulking there for, yer good-for nothing? Come out wi' ye,' and he prodded him with his stick. Charley shot out of the door.

There was a clatter on the stairs as Beth came down at full speed. 'It's gone!' she panted, amazed and alarmed.

'Confound you, the Devil take you – you mean you haven't got the money – you knew it all the time!'

'Begging thy pardon sir, indeed I did not. It was ready for

thee in a box. My brother John must have moved it. We will bring it to thy house immediately he comes home.'

'Ten thousand hells, who the devil do you think you are, that you should not pay your rent like any other Christian?'

'Thou shalt have it for certain sir.'

Just at that moment the door opened. Beth hurried forward. 'Oh John, I'm so glad thou hast come. Where hast thou put the 'Hidey' Box?'

'I?' said John amazed; 'Is it not in its usual place sister?' Beth shook her hed as they stared blankly at each other. Bailiff Foggarty's lips twisted in a triumphant sneer and he spat noisily into the fire. Here was the opportunity to do what he had wanted for a twelvemonth – turn them out. He stood towering above them and spotted the chicken John had brought.

'So this is how the poor live!' He screwed up his eyes and drew his thick brows over them as he poked the bird with his stick. 'Amazing how lazy beggars can live like Lords! Stolen I'll be bound!'

This angered John. 'Begging your pardon Bailiff Foggarty, we may be poor, but we have never stolen one thing!'

The Bailiff shrugged his shoulders. 'As it's Christmas, and to show what a good Christian I am, I'll give you till the first day of January – now there's leniency and generosity for yer. The money is to be paid to me by that day. If not, two of my men will be here – they will take all you possess and you will be OUT! I have given you good warning!' He waved his stick around flicking down some of the greenery. 'I don't know what the likes of you heathens want Christmas decorations for! Chickens – bah!' And he gave the iron pot a ringing bang. Flinging his cloak round him, he made for the door, bumping into one of the wooden joint-stools as he went. His hat was on one side as he bent to rub his shin. 'A plague on me gouty leg – and a plague on you too,' he shouted as he banged the door and was gone.

Beth was in despair. 'There must be some explanation.' John was completely puzzled.

'Are you sure it is not on the ledge?'

'Quite sure,' Beth replied. 'I felt all the way along it.'

John went up and felt also. There was certainly nothing there except cobwebs and dust.

At that moment Charley burst excitedly through the door shouting at the top of his voice, 'They're back! They're back! They're back!' and following him in were Martha and Sammy – Martha, smiling and happy, her arms full of parcels and bags, and Sammy, waving his arms and head from side to side, making all sorts of weird noises and jumping from one foot to the other.

'Martha!' cried Beth flinging her arms round her. 'Do come by the fire – you must be frozen!'

'My goodness yes,' said Martha, 'that was indeed a cold journey – but it is wonderful to see you all again. I promised I'd be back for Christmas didn't I? I see you've been busy decorating the house, and what's this – a chicken! Now listen to what I have planned.' She went chattering on.

'Perhaps John and Charley will help me with some of these bags and then tomorrow – Christmas Day – we'll spend all together. I'll bring some good things to eat and we'll have a wonderful time.' Martha was so happy to be back, and they so happy to see her, they hadn't the heart to tell her all their troubles just then.

Christmas morning dawned, crisp and bitterly cold. Everything outside, trees bushes, roofs and chimneys, were covered with a fresh blanket of snow. Icicles, quite two feet long, hung from the eaves, but the sun was shining and the Christmas bells were ringing. Beth, in her best white coif and pinner, rubbed the frost patterns off the small diamond panes and looked enviously at the families, fathers, mothers, children, all in their Sunday best, laughing gaily together as they went up the road to church and to visit their relations. They all had their families. She wished with all her heart that her father could have been with them for Christmas. She felt very isolated sometimes, for as Puritans they were 'different', and treated with the same suspicion as the 'witch' by the church-going community.

And now this last blow to fall on them was a heavy one. There was no possible way they could get enough money for the rent before the day came when they would be turned out. What would become of them? What could they do? Would they have to go to the Parish workhouse, or worse still, tramp round the countryside begging for food and sleeping where they could? Somehow her mind went to the old 'witch' and she wondered what had really happened to her. She had put her little 'packet' in the 'Hidey' Box and had forgotten it when she was worried about John's arm and Charley's illness. She thought of it now, but *now* was no good. They were certainly in dire need of money, but the Box had gone – where and how? – that was the great cloud hanging over them.

Maybe the 'witch' was only a crazy old woman and probably the packet contained nothing but a few stale herbs – although her words about Owen Ragford were true for he had indeed been a good friend to them. And then the Witch's words came back to her – Don't cross bridges before you come to them' – she knew now what she meant. Many a time she had worried about something and it had all come right in the end. And her other words, 'Look after today and tomorrow will look after itself,' – that was so close to Beth's feelings at the moment.

It was Christmas morning, Christ's birthday. Surely He meant them to enjoy today as much as they could and she had done her best to make it a happy one. A large heap of logs and fir cones stood by the hearth ready to pile the fire up high. The chicken John had brought was soon to go into the iron pot and she had managed to buy six real candles from the chandler – their light was so much better than the ones she made by dipping rushes into fat. Oh, and then the highlight of the day –Martha and Sammy were coming to have dinner with them, and Beth knew, good cook that Martha was, there would be something special in that basket of hers when she did come. She would do, therefore, as the 'witch' bade her, enjoy today and leave tomorrow to look after itself.

So she placed the platters round the table with the wooden spoons and the knives (warning Charley not to touch their sharp points) the earthenware mugs and a jug of ale. The coarse brown bread in the oven by the side of the fire, would come out later. John, however, was still very worried about the rent and decided, Christmas morning though it was, he would go and ask their good friend, Owen Ragford, for his advice. But Owen, his wife said, was not at home, nor was she quite sure when he would be.

Very despondent, he made his way back. If only he could find the 'Hidey' Box. He had turned it over and over in his mind a thousand times. Who could have taken it? Who could possibly have known where it was? He was miserable and cold as he reached home and lifted the wooden latch.

But he could not be too miserable for long. During his absence, Martha and Sammy had arrived and on the table were all the good things she had brought, butter, cheese, eggs, apples, a venison pasty the cook at the Manor House had given her that morning, gingerbread and tarts, elderberry wine she had made herself and a very special Christmas pie made of minced meat, eggs, sugar, raisins, orange and lemon peel and spices.

'Merry Christmas! Merry Christmas! Merry Christmas!' they all cried together, and Sammy clapped his hands and hopped from one foot to the other and clapped them again.

'Come and use the bellows John and thee'll soon be warm,' said Beth, as John, blue with cold, stamped his feet and blew on his nails.

Before long the fire was leaping up the wide chimney and it crackled merrily as they hung the iron pot, filled with herbs and vegetables and the precious chicken, over the flames. The dinner would not be ready for some time, so Beth went upstairs and came down looking very mysterious, holding something behind her. John and Charley knew what it was but they pretended not to, and they all cried, 'Hurray!' as Beth shyly gave them and Sammy a muffler each. They tied them round their necks or put them over their heads as they danced round the table.

Martha knew nothing about the pomander ball and was delighted. 'It will give a pleasant smell for years,' she smiled. Then they all crowded round the fire and cooked apple fritters in the long-handled pan and drank sips of Martha's wine heated in the skillet.

Suddenly they heard voices, the stamping of feet outside and a banging at the door. Beth jumped up, alarmed. Could that be Bailiff Foggarty again? Had be forgotten his promise? The latch was lifted.

To their utter amazement, there stood Owen Ragford and with him - oh, miracle of miracles - their father! The three children rushed to meet him and six arms led him to the settle and sat him down amid a buzz of surprise and delight. Thin and tired after a year and an illness in gaol, but so happy to be

The latch was lifted.
To their utter amazement, there stood Owen Ragford and with him . . . oh, miracle of miracles . . . their father!

home, he looked around him, holding out two hands to them all, which everyone wanted to grasp, including Martha and Sammy. Owen explained he had heard from London, that Cromwell's first Parliament was about to grant the 'Agreement to the People' Act, which would free all dissenters and give them liberty to worship as they pleased, so he had been to see the prison authorities in Northampton on Nathaniel's behalf. They had a high regard for him and were only too glad that so fine a man could be released.

How had they got home everyone wanted to know.

'Well,' Owen explained, 'I went to see Sir Aldwig DuVayne at the Manor and told him what I intended to do and how I wanted it to be a surprise for you all on Christmas Day. He immediately insisted that his coachman, Jonah Marsh, should drive me there and bring us both back.'

Nathaniel grasped Owen's hand and shook it heartily.

'I know thou art a strong churchman, but I also know thou art a good Christian and have been a true friend to my little family this year past. I thank thee with all my heart Brother Ragford.'

'I know thou art a bad Puritan,' said Owen. His eyes twinkled and his pointed beard and moustaches wriggled up an down in that funny sort of way Beth knew so well, 'but you have courage to do what you think is right and I honour you for it Brother Ponder.' He picked up his sugar-loaf hat. 'Well, I must go – it *is* Christmas Day and my wife will be chiding me with neglect of her.'

One hand was on the door latch, the other in the large pocket of his great-coat. 'Bless me!' he cried, 'I almost forgot in the excitement; when I was at the Manor, Squire Aldwig gave me this – it has 'N. PONDER' branded underneath and he thought it must be yours.'

They could hardly believe their eyes. It was the 'Hidey' Box! Beth burst into tears.

'It has been lost father,' John explained, 'and Bailiff Foggarty said he would turn us out if we couldn't pay by New Year's Day.' They all gathered round as he fetched the key and put it into the little hole. Turning it three times forward and twice back, released its hidden spring, and he lifted the lid. 'Nothing is missing – the money is all there! We can pay the rent!' What happiness and relief there was in his voice. 'And here too, Beth, is the packet Mistress Stephens gave you!'

Amid all the rejoicing, Charley had disolved under the table – his favourite place when anything was wrong – wondering fearfully what would happen to him now. 'But how did Squire DuVayne get the box?' was what they all wanted to know.

'Well,' Owen explained, 'the Bailiff's son, Faulk Foggarty was suspected of stealing at the Manor. A search revealed this was true, and among the stolen articles recovered was this box, which Sir Aldwig did not recognise and wondered whose it was till he spotted your name underneath. Nobody was able to open it, least of all young Foggarty, so it is all untouched.'

'Yes, but how did Faulk Foggarty get it? He has never been in our house.' John was baffled.

Then Beth had an idea. 'Charley, do you know anything about this? Charley! Where are you? What are you doing under the table? You *do* know something!'

Very shamefaced, Charley came out, and so did the whole story.

'It was very wicked of you not to tell us.' Beth was really angry.

'I thought it was only an old box that was no good,' he wailed.

'Well, you have it now,' said Owen trying to pour oil on troubled waters. 'It's Christmas Day, and as Master Shakespeare says, All's Well That Ends Well". Yuletide blessings on you – and look after your little family, Brother Ponder – a shoemaker should stick to his last – John is a fine boy and will make a great apothecary one day – your little Beth will be a wonderful wife to some lucky swain, and as for that young rascal Charley, if you'll give me leave to use my birch now and again, we'll have him up to Oxford yet!'

'And we'll promise to convert thee, Brother Ragford, if you'll come to some of our meetings!'

Owen shook his head and laughed. His eyes twinkled and his pointed beard and moustaches wriggled up and down. 'More than my job's worth, Brother Ponder. Happy Christmastide to you all – I do believe it's snowing again!' He pulled up the collar of his great-coat, waved them farewell, and was gone.

They sat happily round the fire, Beth on the rushes at her

father's feet with his hand resting on her red-gold hair. She was still unable to believe all this was true. It seemed as if she had awakened from a bad dream. 'Father,' she said shyly, 'hast thee noticed I have made thee a patchwork cushion for thy settle?'

He had, but had said nothing. Now he got up to have a better look, and everybody waited to see what he would say. He smiled and shook his head. 'What does the Bible say?' he said, ' Vanity of vanities, all is vanity". I think it is too grand for a Puritan's cottage.'

'But father, I made it for thy comfort.'

'And it shall stop there my little Marybud.' He cleared his throat and sat down again. 'Now I have another surprise for you.'

Could there possibly be another surprise on this wonderful day? He was looking fondly at Martha and she at him. 'You are going to have a new mother – Martha and I are going to be married! She has visited me many times at Northampton during the last few months.'

This was indeed a thunderbolt. Beth could hardly believe her ears. Her mouth dropped open in amazement. There was nothing in the whole wide world that could have made her happier. It was so wonderful she thought she *must* be dreaming. She got up, her eyes shining, and threw her arms round Martha's neck, and she in turn embraced and kissed her, and then Beth and Charley and Sammy all jumped round the table for sheer joy. John was laughing.

'Bless me,' he cried, 'Bailiff Foggarty will have his way even now, for we shall have to leave this cottage – it won't be big enough for six of us!'

'*If* Master Foggarty is *still* Bailiff,' said Martha, 'for if I know Squire, he'll have him out neck and crop after this.'

The short December day was pulling in, so the candles were lighted, all six of them, and they and the firelight sent dancing shadows on their happy faces, on the ivy and the holly, with its gay red berries, and on the iron pot whose contents were now filling the room with a delicious aroma. They were getting a bit sleepy by the warm fire, till John's voice roused them with a start. 'Father!' he cried excitedly, 'I've just been opening a packet the old 'witch', Mistress Stephens, gave to Beth.' They crowded round.

'It's only a dirty old piece of paper with some writing on,' said Charley as he peered over John's shoulder.

'Canst thou read it?' asked Nathaniel.

'That I can – almost I think – Dr Cogan will be excited about this – it is a recipe for 'Venice Treacle' – that is something he has been trying to get from Joanna Stephens for years. I know that he offered her a high price, for it is a sure remedy for many ills, but she would never sell.'

'What does it say?' they all wanted to know.

John read slowly as he tried to decipher the faded words. Soak live vipers in white wine, thicken the liquid with honey and liquorice, and then there's a long list of spices and herbs and something, it's difficult to read – about human skulls. I will take it to Dr Cogan as soon as Christmas is over. This will mean a large sum of money for you Beth.'

'Not just for me John, but for us all,' she replied happily, and then she added, 'Poor Mother Stephens – she was indeed a wise old woman. It has been a hard year father, without ye, and I'm afraid I did not always remember to talk to God as thee bade me, but He has helped and looked after us.'

'Beth – my Beth,' Nathaniel looked at her fondly. 'I know something thou hast always remembered – to be courageous, and above everything, kind. We are all saplings in God's garden. He gives us food and water but He is a skilful, loving gardener and knows that he must bend, cut, yes, and almost break sometimes, to make the perfect tree. Thou art a finer sapling now, my Beth, than ever thou wert a year ago.' And as she sat on the rushes, he put his hand on the red-gold hair and said softly, 'We all are my little Marybud.'

Beth's happiness was complete.

The chicken was cooked to a nicety and they gathered chattering round the table. 'Wilt thou say a Grace Beth?' her father asked.

They put their hands together and bowed their heads. She hesitated. Then something both Owen Ragford and the old 'witch' had said to her in their different ways, came back. 'This is the day that the Lord hath made, let us all rejoice and be thankful for it.'

And everyone said 'Amen' to that, before they set about attacking every last scrap of food on the table.